# SPECTACLE OF THE

# EXTENSION

<u>Books by Andy Reynolds</u>

*Spectacle of the Extension*

*The Axeboy's Blues*
*[The Agents Of :: Volume I ::]*

*Visions from the Dream Gyre*
*[Short Stories & Poems]*

# SPECTACLE OF THE

# EXTENSION

ANDY REYNOLDS

# SPECTACLE OF THE EXTENSION

## ANDY REYNOLDS

Published by Mosquito Publishing
ISBN-13: 978-1513624532
ISBN-10: 1513624539

Cover Art by Julia Y   (JuliaY.com)
Author Photo by Mars

First Printed: 2013
Second Edition: 2018

Find out more about Andy's writings at:  AndyReynolds.net
& also:  Facebook.com/AndyWritings

Read tiny slices of his poetry:  Twitter.com/AndyWritings

This book is dedicated to creativity
& the events that shape us,
even when those events are dark & haunting -
for those are often what make a person
beautiful & bright.

# chapter 1

I was the water. I was the wind. All of me was pale to the point of vanishing – pale and flat and smooth. The ocean that was me quivered and black lines emerged from deep within, rising out of the white water like the outline of continents, up into the white sky. The lines grew strong and thick, breathing my air into their lungs, filling themselves out and uncurling into the empty space like stretching cats. I beckoned more of them up to the surface and above it, a snake charmer playing their tune. Inside my space they all curved into each other like sleepy newborn young leaning into their mother to nurse. When the lines touched they created symbols together, some strange and ancient alphabet that had never come into use.

A voice echoed across the water, racing along with the wind; but words meant nothing in that place – only movement and shape held value. Again the voice came, and the lines began to shake and crumble, large sections breaking off and crashing into the pale ocean. The wind howled and the waves roared. I was no longer the wind, nor the water: I was something affected by them, torn at by them. I yanked myself back, like pulling my head from a bucket of ice water, and breathed in.

A sheet of paper lying in front of me, two small hands to either side of it, one of them holding a pen. Shapes were drawn over its surface.

"Earth to Em. You there, girl?"

Looking up from the back counter I saw Meesha standing at the register with a few customers in front of her, all of them looking my way.

"Um, yeah." Maybe I shouldn't get so into my drawings at work. It had just been so damned slow that night, and I'd almost figured out what my painting was missing. This painting had been consuming my creative life for months now, and it was sitting there alone in my apartment, unfinished. It had taken over my thoughts, my dreams – but over the last couple of weeks nothing that I added to the piece was quite right. I'd been so very close for so long now that it was starting to drive me nuts. I just wanted to be done with it so I could move on to whatever was next.

Meesha sang an order to me quasi-operatically. "*Latte,*" she sang, then, "*Medium. Hazelnut.*" She swiveled where she stood to face the small cluster of customers across the counter from her.

I pulled myself up from the back counter, yawned and checked the clock on the wall. 11:45. Almost time to close up shop.

When I'm not *the water and the wind* I tend to be five-foot-three, twenty-four years old and have short black hair sticking up every which-way. Sometimes I wear shirts and dresses that I make from the stuff I find at thrift stores – I cut them apart and sew them back together to make them more interesting. Dressing that way got me the nickname "scarecrow" back in high school, but no one here knows me by that name, which suits me just fine.

Meesha sang a couple more orders to me and I began making the drinks, letting the high-pitched roar of the steaming milk drown out the godawful bubblegum-chewing-teen-whining-about-how-no-one-understands-her electronica that Meesha always put on before we closed. Closing with Luke was easier on the nerves; he usually mixed it up between jazz and hardcore punk, switching back and forth mid-song when we were in the last ten-minute stretch. "Don't let them get too comfortable," he'd always say. "We can't let them forget their worries. Not completely." As if the manipulation of the coffee shop's music was part of some grandiose social experiment to him, a way to subtly shape and evolve human consciousness.

I handed the drinks off to the customers and looked over my drawing when Meesha walked over. "Come on, Em. Heads or tails?"

"Why do you ask me that?"

She huffed. Her curly red hair was like an overstuffed halo around her head. She was a goofy looking girl, yet her almond eyes and creamy skin gave an exotic edge to her appearance. Unfortunately the way she wore her hair caused the goofy part to overshadow the exotic. "I ask you because of tradition."

"I'm gonna pick machine and you're gonna pick mop."

She flipped the coin in the air, caught it and slapped it onto her

arm. "Call it, or face the aftermath of bad luck."
"Heads."
She checked. "It's heads. Mop or machine?"
"Machine."

*      *      *

I loved the espresso machine. I'd been working at *The Cove* for two years, ever since I'd moved to the city after art school, and even when things were bad and I couldn't bring myself to paint, even when all the events of my life seemed to lead up to this point of nothingness that I couldn't see past, I could work on the machine and feel that on some level I and the machine were the same thing. When I cleaned the machine, I was cleaning myself – getting the gunk out, flushing chemicals through it, then polishing the surfaces until they shined (or at least I *told* the espresso machine that it shined; really it looked like something that would be lying out on a blanket at a yard sale – but hey, it made damned fine coffee). I wouldn't think while I cleaned it, not anymore. In that way cleaning it was similar to the way I wanted to paint – to just move and create from something within and not be bogged down with symbolism and color schemes, to delete the years of art school teachers jabbering on and on in my head every time I picked up a brush.

"So, Em, what've you been working on so studiously over there?"

I stood on my tiptoes and peered over the machine at her as she mopped the lobby, then sunk back down. "It's this painting I've been working on. I think I've almost figured out what it needs."

"Is that all you do when you're not working? Paint?"

I started wiping off the back counters. "Painting is my real job. When I'm not doing my real job, I hang out here and make drinks for people. Or I watch movies. Or read."

"I wish I painted or played music or something. I'm so ordinary."

"I read an article about this guy who'd never done anything creative. He got into meditation, emptied out a room in his house and sat in it for days, just staring at the wall. Then something in his head snapped and he started inventing all kinds of things. Ended up winning all these awards, even the Nobel Prize I think. He loved inventing so much that he never stopped."

"Thanks for rubbing it in that I'm ordinary, Em."

"I meant it more as an inspiration."

Meesha laughed. "Hey, I'm meeting up with some friends over at Neptune after we close. You should come. I'll buy you a drink. That way if my friends don't show at least I won't be there drinking by myself."

The word *no* reverberated around in my head, but then my eyes fell on the sketch I'd been working on. It was alright, but not even close to the emotion I was trying to pry out of my head. I thought of the canvas and easel in the middle of my empty apartment, and felt like I'd just get depressed if I went home. "Sure, why not?" I crumpled up the paper and tossed it into the trash.

                    *          *          *

The Cove, where I worked, was in a small outdoor mall called The Island which was designed to look like a post-apocalyptic town from the late 1800s, complete with gas lamps and cobblestone sidewalks with fake trolley tracks and beautiful, broken-looking buildings. There's an ongoing rumor that it's based on an old book, but when I read the book there was nothing about an island or a town being blown up. I can't even remember what the book's called now. The clothing stores in The Island were kind of trendy, but occasionally had something of interest on the clearance rack. There was also a music store, a book shop and a hair salon. Most of the places had names which related to islands or water.

The bar called Neptune was in another outdoor mall across the street called The System (as in *solar* system), which was either an architect's vision of the future or their vision of what an alien mall would look like. The buildings were strange and angular, covered in murals of stars and planets and black holes, with multi-colored spotlights criss-crossing all the walkways. The end result was more like a Spanish mission on a mild acid trip than anything from space. The System had a few restaurants, a camping supply store and a scuba diving training facility, which would have made more sense to have at The Island. All of the places were named after planets, star systems or other space paraphernalia.

It was a Tuesday night and Neptune was nearly empty. The bartender greeted Meesha by name, and she asked for a vodka cran.

Meesha raised an eyebrow when I ordered a Stoli Black

Russian. "That's not what I'd pictured you drinking."

She looked kind of attractive in the dimness of the bar – I bet she got a lot of one night stands. It wasn't like she'd have to work hard to look pretty - she *was* pretty. But something about her confidence was off, and it showed. Not to mention that damned goofiness.

She looked down at her green fingernails. "Actually, I don't think I've ever seen anyone *order* a Black Russian."

The bartender sat the drinks down. Hers was pink and mine was almost black. It was fitting. She raised her glass and I touched mine to hers and we drank.

"So, what's 'Em' stand for, anyway? Emma?"

"I wish. It stands for Emily."

"There's nothing wrong with 'Emily.' You don't seem like one, though."

"I guess I liked the name when I was little. It just doesn't fit me anymore."

"I used to think people should be able to re-pick their names. Maybe when they're twelve or fourteen."

"That could only end badly." I took a long drink. My body relaxed into the bar stool as the alcohol started its work on me.

"Yeah. I guess that's why I stopped thinking about it."

"Anyway, I like being Em. And I wouldn't be an Em if I hadn't first been Emily."

"True, true."

Since I rarely drank at Neptune I wasn't sure if the drinks were usually so stiff, or if the bartender was hooking us up because Meesha knew them. Halfway through my second Black Russian I found the conversation dissolving into gossip about coworkers, a degradation I pride myself in never lapsing into. Then Meesha was getting this big glassy-eyed look to her, like she was about to hit on me, and I didn't know her well enough to know if she would or not. I finished my drink and made a polite retreat just in case. Glancing back at the bar as I left, seeing her sitting there alone and hunched over her drink – not like someone in their early twenties, but like someone much, much older – something occurred to me: she never had any friends coming, and she'd have gone there with me or without. I wished I was better with people, so that maybe I could help her, talk to her, see why she was depressed and hid it from everyone behind that goofy smile.

No, that's a lie – I had no wish to console her. I just wanted to paint and be left alone.

As I walked past the depictions of black holes and stars, through vertical beams of red and green light, I realized out loud, "I don't care about anyone."

## chapter 2

The disorganized room had a peculiar odor to it, a tapestry of smell woven together from threads of take-out food and styrofoam, of paints and alcohols and paint thinner. I am uncertain of just how long I was bathed in awareness before realizing that I had obtained some form of independent existence. Or, rather, that I had obtained an awareness *of* such an existence. Actually, it would be more accurate to state that I had obtained both existence and awareness *of* said existence simultaneously, as if the two went hand in hand – if one of them were to leave, the other would wither away like a lonely lover, without purpose, without a reason to be.

Standing there, looking up at me, was the young lady who's name was etched onto every shred of my being – Em. It didn't occur to me at the time to wonder how I knew her name, but apart from my own existence it seemed the only thing that I knew. She was holding in her hand a glass of black liquid and ice. In the other hand was clutched a brush, its tip dripping with dark blue-violet blood. A paint-splattered table stood tall at her side, on which was placed various jars and plastic cups of paints and liquids. Her thick black hair was short and sticking up sporadically, and her two eyes were exact copies of the black, glassy ice cubes floating in her drink. The dark violet-blue blood ran up both of her arms and covered the backs of her frail hands. It was my blood. I looked down at myself and it was all over me.

I tried leaning forward, but found myself incapable. Like I was chained down. She reached out and smeared the brush across me, across my flatness, and a bout of emotions bubbled up inside of me: the urge to hold her, to fly up into the air, to turn myself inside out or to rip something apart. Then another stroke of her hand and I stretched out, feeling every inch of my body from the center to the

ANDY REYNOLDS

outer edges. I felt things growing from me, and short, black feathers began sprouting from my surface, bursting from my blood-splattered flesh like welts. It burned, but I felt so alive!

I roared out! I screamed into the small room! Madness would surely take me if I was bound for any longer. How could I exist in such a way?

Then the universe heeded my call – I was released. Rising up to the ceiling, I breathed the room deep into my being. Below me, that frail creature moved the bloody brush across a canvas. Was I that canvas down there? Then how could I be so far up here, worlds away? I twisted through the air, my blood-soaked and feathered body bending and flexing in the empty space of the room.

Lowering down behind her, I watched over her shoulder as she painted. Yes, it looked just like me, didn't it? Such a likeness. Then I looked down at my own body. She almost had it; she was so close. A few more feathers, a slightly different shape. Reaching around her neck, I touched her chin and tilted her head back gently, then rose up above her, looking down into her eyes. She knew me. She made me. Yet she could not see me.

I opened my mouth and something akin to a tongue came out and I licked the center of her forehead, from which sprouted dozens of tiny violet feathers. Her mouth opened and she cried out, her eyes wide, and for a second I knew that she saw me there, floating above her like a blue cloud riddled with violet lightning.

Her glass shattered on the concrete floor and she braced herself against the table. The tiny feathers on her forehead twitched and breathed in the room like antennae. Then she touched the blood-soaked brush against the canvas. Each and every movement of the brush brought to my own mind and body further sustenance and solidity, and with every stroke the very room around us harnessed more definition for me, and I could see her even more clearly – her tiny bare feet covered in small shards of glass and drops of alcohol, her face glowing and almost see-through.

We both knew when the last stroke was being dealt: it was like a long sigh rising up through the core of my being, and her hand moved so terribly slow, as if she wanted that last stroke to go on forever. Then the brush slipped from her hand and clattered to the ground. Something on her face caught the light, and a single tear slid down her cheek. She grabbed a knife from the table, cut off a long, thin pinch of her hair and dipped the strands into a cup of deep red paint. Without the slightest hesitation, she named me. She wrote my name in the corner.

Ah, yes. I knew it then, as if it had always been so. That's who I was.

My name was W.

# chapter 3

I opened one eye and saw the apocalypse. It looked a lot like my room, except messier and covered in a searing white light that reached through my one eye and stabbed at my brain with a rusted sword. I closed my eye and begged for dreams to steal me away from my body and its need to pee, but dreams had already had their way with me and thought nothing of leaving me to my self-inflicted demise.

My body rolled off the futon mattress and thumped onto the floor. I pushed myself up, my muscles trying to stage a coup against me, and steadied myself on the wall as I made my way to the bathroom. Maybe they had a right to stage a coup – it's not like I ever took their interests to heart. Afterwords I drank three glasses of water, feeling my body becoming a little closer to normal with each gulp.

I saw it when I walked out of the bathroom. "Oh my god..." I tried to remember how the painting had gotten there. I saw my style inside of it, but I'd never painted anything so good. It robbed the space around it of any color, commanded a presence that furiously sucked the details out of the rest of the room. I was looking at something better than I. Something I had created was more real than I was.

Looking down at my hands, I saw the dried and cracked evidence all over me. On the floor in front of the painting was a circle of broken glass and sticky brown alcohol, with two ovals of clean floor where my feet had been. I checked my feet, but except for drops of dried Kahlua and paint they were completely unscathed. I couldn't look away from the painting for more than a few seconds, and for the first time in my life I really felt the need for a cigarette. Maybe it was time to start up.

I pulled on some pants, grabbed my keys and some cash and went downstairs to the convenience store that I lived above. When I walked outside the sun hit me like a metal bat and I slouched against the brick wall, covering my eyes. I stumbled half-blind into the store.

"Shoes!" yelled Abid from behind the counter.

"Sorry, Abid," I muttered as my eyesight returned. I grabbed a carton of orange juice and took it to the counter.

"You have to wear shoes when you come in here."

"I'll bring some down and keep them behind the counter." I handed him a few dollars, glancing behind him at the rows of cigarettes.

"What are you looking at those for, young lady?" He had the gold-brown eyes of a trickster, like he was always defying something.

"What do people smoke these days? What's good?" I opened the orange juice and took a long drink, then wiped my mouth with the back of my hand.

He raised an eyebrow. "Let me see your ID."

"For what? You're my *vodka* supplier."

Abid shrugged. "I am sorry, I don't remember. You look familiar, but so many people come in and out of my store, it's hard on the mind." He slouched dramatically and took off his glasses, as if even *they* didn't work any longer.

I smirked. "Jerk. I'll be sure to have my mom write you a thank you note."

"Ah, your mother. How is she doing?"

"Still picture perfect, like always." I offered him some orange juice and he shook his head. "She's nice and content in suburbia half a country away."

"Does she know you paint your body while drinking at night?" He motioned to my arms.

I laughed. "I'm sure she would sleep better at night if she believed that's all I did." My eyes fell on my violet-blue hands and I suddenly remembered the painting. "Oh yeah..." My mind was so disorganized, still pulling itself together.

"What? You have the sudden urge to join society and work for a living?"

I laughed and a thin pain shot through my head like an arrow. "Ouch. No, I think I just painted something really good last night. I need to go up and look at it. Make sure I didn't make it up in my head."

"I might recommend that you stay here rather than face the truth and heart ache."

"Jackass." I made my way towards the door. "Keep hitting on the women. It'll work eventually."

"When the social workers come, I will tell them I don't know where you live."

"Thanks."

Distracted, I'd forgotten all about the sun and nearly dropped my orange juice when the gaseous ball of flame jumped me.

*     *     *

I could swear that the painting had grown since I'd been downstairs. It seemed more aware of its surroundings, more sure of itself. I didn't know what to do. I had to paint another one. Well, I'd have to figure out what I did and then do it again. It was exactly what I was trying to get out of me, right there staring me in the face. I wondered if anyone else would be able to see it.

It was only noon, plenty of time before I had to go to work – and I was starving. But first I had to get all that paint off of me. I put on a Bessie Smith CD, swept up the broken glass on the floor and scrubbed my arms in the kitchen sink. Not that I had a kitchen really, just a corner of my apartment that served a similar purpose. I turned on the shower, waltzed with the music over to my bed and threw off my clothes, belting out the lyrics with Bessie. "*Some people call me a hobo, some call me a bum. Nobody knows my name, nobody knows what I've done! I'm as good as any woman in your town.*"

Something caught my eye and I crouched down next to my mattress. Feathers. A handful of small, black feathers were scattered next to my pillow. Weird. Maybe I found them walking home after Neptune. But I wasn't that drunk yet – I should have remembered. I must have gone outside after I'd been drinking and painting, found them in the park.

I looked over my shoulder at the painting. There were feathers lodged into the paint – maybe raven feathers? But the ones on my pillow were different. Maybe it was a full moon or something, and I was just being weird.

My stomach rumbled loudly, letting me know how much it cared about full moons and paintings. I twirled along with Bessie's voice across the room, grabbed the Orange Juice and took a long swig, then sauntered into the bathroom and stepped into the shower.

chapter 4

Water slapping against porcelain thousands upon thousands of times a second. A woman singing through electronics about being sad or about how it's alright for her to sleep with several men or about a town of people so tough that they'd use gunpowder to sweeten their tea. These were the sounds that occupied the room along with me. I was thin, pressed up against the corner above the mattress like a city of cobwebs. When I touched the walls I would get overwhelmed – all the molecules trying to speak to me at the same time. So I hung there, static. I had a name now, but what was my purpose? Perhaps I didn't need a purpose, or perhaps *she* would give me one.

Instead of touching the walls, I smelled them. Paint and brick and wood, wrapped into an uneasy alliance. They were tired, but would hold together a while longer if that's what was asked of them.

The water stopped running and I watched her dry off through the open bathroom door. She looked small enough to hold, like a bird – so innocent and frail. Like she could be crushed by the wind. Yet she had spawned me, and the emotions which sifted through my being bound me to her, just as all my thoughts were directed like arrows in her direction.

I wanted to follow her, to know her.

She came out of the bathroom and spun across the room, nearly tripping on a box of clothes sitting in the middle of the floor, then kicked the box to the side. I left the wall, moving slowly through open space. She seemed completely unaware of my existence, yet she kept glancing at the painting of me. I lowered down behind her and smelled the air just above the back of her neck. It was moist with scents of lavender and soap and a slight hint of coffee. She bowed her head forward and closed her eyes. I swam down and around her, peering up into her face.

I wanted to reach out and touch her, but was uncertain of what that would do to me when I couldn't even handle touching the wall. Then her eyes opened and she looked right through me with those black jewels. She touched her hand to the skin above her heart, and it was as if she were asking me to touch her there as well. Her face was so very serene. I reached out with a shaking hand, and when my body touched hers the room softly melted into light.

Her skin was glowing, and I felt the thumping of her organs gently but firmly resounding through my head. All of my questions, my anticipations, they all evaporated, leaving me with such a vast and empty peace. She stepped backwards, away from me, and when my hand slipped away from hers the room returned. Floating up to the ceiling, a strange calm had taken me, and I watched as she dressed and went about making food for herself. Then she gathered a sketchbook and some things into a shoulder bag and went to leave.

I swam down and grabbed onto the bag, letting her pull me out the door.

*          *          *

At first the world outside was almost too big for me. I'd seen it out the window, and I remembered it as if from a dream, but in person it was so large and proud and bright. So many creatures scurrying around everywhere, some in vehicles, some with wings or tiny legs. There were really old ones standing tall with their branches up in the sky. I wanted to go back into the apartment, but the thought of such a frail being as Em out alone in this frighteningly busy world kept me latched onto her bag. I didn't know how I could possibly help her if she became threatened, but I couldn't leave her alone in such chaos.

She pulled me through the massive stone archway which served as the entrance to a park, the giant oak trees bowing and nodding to us as we passed underneath them. She stopped several times to sit down and sketch the mighty bark-covered creatures, and eventually we made our way through the park and out onto a large, busy street. Overgrown metal vehicles streamed past, creating clashing whirlwinds of noise, and I was forced to look away or be visually overloaded. She pulled me down the sidewalk, and then, as if they too realized her majesty, the monstrous metallic machines all stopped, creating a pathway which led from where she stood to the other side of the street. She stepped out in front of them casually, taking her time as she crossed, as if the beasts were nothing and could wait all day if that's how long she felt like taking. I looked at them as they sat there vibrating, and through the windshields the people inside them looked so docile and content, so lost in their minds and not lost at all in the world around them or in their passions.

How? How could they possibly be so passionately distracted from their passions? How could they be blind to the amazing chaotic danger and beauty that lies just inches from the walls of their skin? What kind of world was this, and who were its strange inhabitants?

# chapter 5

When I got to work it was slammed. I bumped my way past the hoards, slid behind the counter and past the new girl Molly who was working the register, and threw my bag down. "What's your status?" I asked Luke, who was making drinks on the espresso machine.

"Hey, it's the Emster," he said as he pulled the small fridge open with the toe of his shoe.

I analyzed the contents and went to the back, returning with four gallons of milk, two hanging from each hand, and sliding them in. I helped through the rush, did some damage-control cleanup and then it was time for Molly to leave. Almost all the tables were full, but there was no line.

"You're good to go, Mole," said Luke.

I elbowed him as Molly took off. "Luke! You don't call a girl 'Mole.' Just 'cause you wear those goofy flannels and don't brush your hair doesn't mean you can go around offending people."

Luke shrugged. "I asked her, she likes it. I gave her a choice of nicknames."

"Like what?"

"Mole. Moly." He ran a hand through his disheveled hair. "Would have offered Emster if it wasn't already taken."

"Well, don't call her Mole again. You'll make her quit. Hey, you get off at seven, right?"

"Yep."

"You mind coming over after? I want to show you a new painting."

"Not tonight. The old lady's dragging me to some kinda puppet-show-slash-stage-play-slash-orchestra shindig."

"Luke, when you break her heart and leave her crying in the middle of the street, could you give her my number?"

"Will do." He suddenly looked taken aback. "I think that's her calling, I better step into the back and get this." He pulled his phone out of his pocket and rushed off without even a glance at the phone. What the hell?

I turned around and saw one of our regulars, a guy that Luke had gotten half of our coworkers to refer to as my "boyfriend," walking up to the register. Now Luke's departure made sense. The guy was pale with shaggy black hair and bright green eyes, and had his hands in the pockets of a black corduroy jacket. "Hey," he said to me, which is about all he ever said to me besides, "Could I get a medium latte?"

"Medium latte?" I asked.

He nodded. "Please."

I grabbed a cup and walked over to the espresso machine. As far as I knew he barely talked to anyone, but he always looked at me like we were both members of the same secret society – like we both knew something that no one else did. I've had guys who were too shy to talk to me before, but this guy was different. It's like he wasn't afraid of talking to me, he just *chose* not to, which I figured was a cop-out and it just pissed me off. I felt like every time he ordered a latte from me he was just wasting both our times. Not that I wanted him to ask me out or anything, I really didn't care – I just wished he would stop being so half-assed.

Before I realized how annoyed I was, I'd slammed the drink down in front of him. "Sorry," I said quickly. "I didn't mean to slam that down."

He looked a little worried. "I – I haven't paid yet."

"Uh, don't worry about it today," I said and walked into the back room.

"Um, thanks!"

I leaned back against a wall next to Luke, who was playing a game on his cell phone. "Ghaa! He's infuriating!"

"*Love's a strange creature,*" he sang. "Don't steal that, I made it up I think."

"You play bass. Bassists can't write lyrics, remember? I'm sure you stole it from someone. Billy Holiday maybe."

"Ouch. You're really worked up over this guy, huh?" He slipped his phone into his pocket and peeked his head out. "I can take him out to the alley, show him some manners."

"Forget it," I said and walked back out. The guy was sitting across the room like usual, powering on his laptop, large headphones straddling his head. I rinsed out the milk pitcher, grabbed the newspaper from the day before and skimmed through it.

*        *        *

Rain came down outside and business stayed pretty slow. It was halfway through my shift and I'd just finished making a round of drinks when my heart started pounding like a war drum. I touched my chest and closed my eyes, and everything grew very quiet except for my heart. I thought I might pass out, and forced my eyes open. The espresso machine was something else at that moment – it was alive and reaching towards me. I felt it pulling at my chest, at my insides, as if it wanted to drag me into itself. My hand shot out and pressed against it for balance, and the metal and plastic vibrated into my skin, the molecules of my hand and the machine dancing with each other, switching places. I yanked my hand away and for a split second I swore that half my palm was made of stainless steel, and then it was skin again.

I looked around but no one seemed to have witnessed my weird spell. Luke was off sitting at a table and talking to a friend; everyone else was engaged in their laptops or books or conversation. Coltrane was on the CD player, and as one song stopped and before the next started, the pelting of the rain on the outside tables was the only noise. There was such an abundance of quiet energy inside of me – I felt it nudging me towards the back room, so I let it guide me back there.

chapter 6

Her eyes locked with mine and I swam backwards into the
storage room. I had pulled at a stream which arose from her chest
like a small, bubbling fountain, and something similar arose from
within myself. The two fountains had met halfway between us and
bubbled into each other, entwining and braiding together like a
sloppy, liquid rope. And now, as I swam backwards into the storage
room, she followed; the fountains stretching thin between us when
the distance grew, refusing to let go of each other.

I pulled Em to the large refrigerator which I'd felt calling to
me, or calling her *through* me, and I watched her gaze at the streaks
of light that stretched across its metallic surface. From behind her I
wrapped my feathered arms around her body, suddenly overtaken by
such an intense and uncontrollable longing, a need to be back inside
of this body-mind of hers from which I came. Intensely alone, I felt
cast out like a cat whose owners had skipped town without it,
leaving it to the dark and rainy streets to either learn how to survive
or to die. I yearned to not know that I was alive again, to not feel
every pore of my skin so acutely, to rest inside this girl who had
spawned me – not as the consciousness that I had become, but as a
mere piece, a sliver of her body's consciousness. Wet, blue liquid
trickled down my face in twin streams, tears pouring forth from my
face like broken spigots. They spilled onto the back of her neck,
onto her shoulders and down her front, soaking into and staining her
shirt. I wished for the fountains to break their bond between us; I
wished for an end to everything that I felt.

The longing in me subsided slightly, and I pushed myself away
from her and watched the blue liquid come alive across her chest
and shoulders, splashing out into the air around her like amorphous
misplaced wings, reaching and breathing.

Her palm slammed against the refrigerator. The lights which were streaked across the metal surface moved and changed form, becoming shapes and things akin to letters. When they finally lay at rest, her free hand shot out towards the manager's desk, and like a boomerang I was flung across the storage room, my hand wrapping around several markers sticking out of a plastic cup, and then I was pulled back. Her eyes never left the refrigerator as my hand was pulled to hers and spontaneously opened. The markers fell as her hand closed, all of them clattering to the ground except the red and the black which she'd caught in her fist. She pulled the caps off with her teeth, spitting them onto the floor, and began tracing over the symbols of light simultaneously with both colors, yet sometimes only the red touched the surface and sometimes only the black. Her head nodded back and forth as her hand glided over the metal surface. The fountains between us unraveled, though still nudged each other like cats in the afternoon sun, the blue tear-liquid stretching slowly in the air around her from each shoulder like the inside of lava lamps.

Floating up to the ceiling, I felt inside my chest the symbols she drew etching themselves into me. They burned like fire, as if I had organs and she was moving the organs around, reshaping them, making them more efficient, more focused. The fire inside me grew more intense and my fountain curled up into me like a proboscis. I wrapped my arms around myself and curled into a ball, but the pain intensified. I let out a wail that shook the walls – every molecule of the building sang out to comfort me, if only to make me stop wailing and leave it in peace.

Then it was done. The symbols were branded across my insides, and it hurt so bad that I couldn't move. I closed my eyes, but could not stop the pain. I heard Em's coworker Luke come into the back.

"Yo, what're you up to?"

"I… I don't know, Luke."

"Wow. That's pretty killer. Boss-man's gonna be pissed, though. You know, every time I see your work after not seeing it for a while, I'm blown away by how much better you've gotten."

"Thanks," Em whispered.

I felt my body starting to break apart. This must be it, I thought. I'm dying. Such utter relief washed over me, that I was going to break up and become part of everything else – yet I also felt bad for Em, for leaving her. But what good was I to her in a state like that? I didn't even know what I was.

I forced my eyes open, saw myself dissipating into the air. I looked down at her as she stared at the red and black drawing, the symbols. "Goodbye," I whispered, and then I was gone.

# chapter 7

I spun around, looking at the shelves packed with coffee and tea and boxes of styrofoam cups. I swore I'd just heard something, someone speaking. Punk music was rocking out in the coffee shop, so I chalked it off to hearing a weird drum beat or a renegade lyric. Looking back at the refrigerator, I felt such a strong connection with the drawing. There'd been this weird feeling in me, something new, and it had reached out through me and drawn itself onto the refrigerator, without me even trying to pull it out of my head. What in the hell was happening to me?

"Yo, Emster!" Luke called from the front. "Customerroes, ten o'clock."

I nearly tripped on some of the markers that were scattered on the floor. What the hell? Did I just do that? I squeezed my temples and took a deep breath, then slapped my cheek. "Come on, Em." Well, the markers would just have to hang out on the floor for a minute.

When I walked out of the storage room, Luke was already making the customers' drinks, so I started ringing them up.

\*　　　\*　　　\*

The rain came down harder and business never really picked up. I occupied myself with the newspaper for a while, trying not to get too pissed off at all the articles about violence and corruption. Thunder boomed above us quite regularly, either making the punk music more chaotic or the jazz music more haunting.

Later, near the end of my shift, I was walking around wiping off tables when the boyfriend guy looked outside at the downpour and took off his headphones.

"Where are you supposed to be?" I asked him.

He looked at me and raised an eyebrow. If he didn't speak to me, I was going to hit him – there was no way around it. It just wasn't a day where I could hold myself back.

"Home. I've done about all I can here. And I have an *appointment*." The way he said "appointment" seemed to imply a hidden meaning – more importantly a meaning that only he and I were privy to. Though of course I had no idea what he meant, so I ignored the comment.

"So, what's your flavor?" I asked him. I got a kick asking people enigmatic questions and seeing what they thought I meant by how they answered.

"Music," he said, then gave his laptop a questioned look. "Kind of. What's yours?"

"Paint. Multimedia."

He smirked. "I've always liked that word: multimedia. I wish it were used for music."

"Music is a media, so it's not exactly 'multi' unless its shown with something else."

"Visual art is a media, yet it's referred to as 'multi' all the time."

"Sure," I said, not in the mood for an altercation. "So you bang on trash cans or splice in recorded conversations with Houdini or… god, you aren't one of those power-tool guys, are you?"

He did his eyebrow-raising thing. "Kind of; something like that; and no, I haven't used power tools in my music up to this point. It's more like –"

"Ah-p," I said, cutting him off. I tried to mimic his weird eyebrow thing. "That's enough for today. Don't want either of us to get over-stimulated." I turned around and walked back across the coffee shop.

Luke was hunched over the newspaper at the front counter. "Didn't hear him scream. You didn't mace him?"

"Left the mace at home," I glanced across the room at the boyfriend guy, who was putting his laptop away while looking out at the rain. "Maybe tomorrow."

"I thought you were off tomorrow."

"Switched with Meesha."

"Well aren't you the little hero."

*       *       *

There was a light rain when my shift ended, and I was more or less soaked by the time I got home. I never minded the rain as long as it wasn't too cold out, and the early autumn air was still warm and thick. My sneakers made squishy sounds when I walked up the stairs to my door, and I imagined the boyfriend guy recording the sound for his music. He could call it "Squishy Shoe Blues."

I opened my door and tossed down my shoulder bag, which I'd wrapped in a plastic grocery bag to protect my drawings. I wrestled off my soggy shoes and socks and sat on the floor with my back to the wall. It was still a little light out. I didn't feel like painting or drinking yet, and there wouldn't be any kind of concerts or other goings-on until later. This was the problem I sometimes faced with working early evening shifts.

Something rattled in the bathroom and I froze.

I looked around me and picked up a nearly empty bottle of Stoli. Holding it upside down by the handle, I quietly got to my feet. The lights were still off; the cloud-covered twilight sifted through the dusty windows as I crept across the room towards the half-closed bathroom door. The front door *had* been locked, hadn't it? I'm sure it had been, and that something just randomly fell in the bathroom. Still, never hurts to be careful.

I took a deep breath, raised the bottle above my head and shoved the door open. In the near-darkness I saw a squirming ball of shadow. I let out a war cry and swung down. A pale, violet face with blue lips and purple-shadowed eyes jerked around to look at me in shock and I half-halted my attack, my war cry catching in my throat as my bottle came down with a thud next to the thing's head. I tried to scream, but was coughing as I fell backwards, scrambling to get away from the strange animal-thing. I half-ran, half-crawled across the room towards the front door, and in a dark blur it was between the door and myself – a mass of dark violet and blue and feathers. It was large, about twice my size.

I had no use for fear then, so I let my fear turn into rage. Then it occurred to me that I was looking at an intruder who had wrapped themselves in my painting, and my rage doubled. I grabbed the knife off my small paint table. "*Get the fuck out,*" I growled. "*Leave the painting. Get out of here.*"

"Em," it said in a soothing, deep voice.

That was it – I grabbed the paint table and threw it. Jars crashed, paint splashed and brushes skittered across the ground. *"Get out!"*

It floated up to the ceiling and I took a step back. My mind was racing. Was it a ghost? It couldn't be, because I'd hit it with a bottle. Can you hit ghosts with bottles? Maybe it was some kind of animal – an animal that knew my name.

"I'm sorry to have frightened you," it said. Its voice sounded kind of like a man's. "But it may console you to know that I am just as taken aback as you."

"Who are you?"

A look of sadness crossed its face. "The name you yourself have crowned me with is W."

"Me myself? Um, I think maybe you have me mixed up with another Em. Now how come you look like my painting?"

"I don't look like your paining – you're painting looks like me. All I know is that I've come from you, that you spawned me. I was hoping to glean more understanding from you. Just hours ago I thought that I had perished. I had no idea you'd ever be able to see me."

I peered into its face. It looked vaguely human, yet the curves were all wrong, and I couldn't make out any eyes underneath the purple-black shadows. Even though it was creepy, somehow it didn't seem aggressive or dangerous, so I went along with it, still holding my knife of course. "Alright, then. When did I name you?"

"Last night, just after I came into consciousness. I'll show you." He drifted over to the painting (which was still there and not wrapped around him) while politely keeping his distance from me, and pointed down to the corner.

"Sorry, but that's an 'M', not a 'W', though I've never signed a painting like that before." The intruder's skin was constantly shifting like it was made of moving blue and violet splotches, and the feathers bowed up and down with its movements. Its hands, like its face, were made of creamy pale-purple skin.

"I thought you knew, but I suppose that makes sense – the way images travel into the eye and get flipped around."

"You mean it's upside down." I tucked the knife into my back pocket, picked up the painting and put it back on the easel upside down. I felt like I was seeing a new painting. The same emotion was there, only it was pushing itself outward instead of sucking energy into itself, and from the mass of dark violets and blues and feathers a soft, distinct face peered out. It was almost hidden in the tempest swirling around it. And up in the corner, scrawled in thin orange-red paint was the letter W. "It's you," I muttered.

W floated down next to me then. "It's also a piece of you," he said. "I'm certain of that."

I walked over and picked up the bottle of Stoli I'd hit him with, unscrewed the cap and took a swig, coughing from the burn of room temperature vodka. I closed my eyes. When I opened them, I realized how dark it was. Turning around, I saw him there, quietly watching me and as he floated next to the painting of him. For the first time, the painting looked insignificant; being right next to the real thing stole away all of its power. "I can hardly see you, but I'm afraid to turn on the light. Afraid you'll vanish, afraid that this is a dream, or that I'm totally nuts."

"I am here," said W. "As surely as you are."

But then he began melding into the shadow around him. "What are you doing?"

"Nothing."

"Why are you going away? I have questions. Stay here!"

I flipped on the light, and even though he was only half there as he melted away, he was even more magnificent. I still couldn't make out his eyes, but I could feel them beneath the violet, drinking me in. He drifted towards me and my hand pressed into a cluster of his feathers. They were even softer than real feathers, but were losing their solidity. He took a deep breath and my hand moved as his chest moved.

"Where are you going?" I asked again.

"I'm not going anywhere, Em," he said, reaching up and touching my hand with his. His hand felt cold and smooth like snake's skin. "I don't think you could get rid of me if you tried."

My hand fell through him, and a few seconds later he was completely gone. I said his name in the empty room, but there was no answer. A sudden loneliness gripped me, of a depth that I hadn't felt for years. I didn't think that I'd been hallucinating. I didn't think that I was crazy. But I also didn't believe that I'd ever see W again.

# chapter 8

After her hand passed through me, leaving trails of blue and violet billowing around her, and it was obvious that she could no longer see me, I let myself up to the ceiling. No longer could I fear anything, for I had met my creator, and her eyes had fallen upon me. She had accepted me. My shoulder throbbed from where the bottle had struck, but the pain was a reminder of our encounter and I was so glad to have it.

Below me, she picked up a glass from the floor, poured clear and black liquid into it and then dropped a few ice cubes inside. Sitting down on the floor in front of the painting of me, she gazed at it, taking long sips. After a while she buried her face in her arms, and I lowered down behind her. I put a hand on her shoulder and kissed the back of her head, but these things had no effect, as if I were not even there.

"Everything's alright," I whispered.

My body: dry, empty. No fountains or feathers or liquids poured forth from me, nor did anything move inside – so it seemed I had no way of affecting her. Maybe that meant she did not want to be affected, since I was a piece of her – for it must be through her that I was empowered, enabled. I moved back to the ceiling, pressed against the paint there, half-listening to the wood and brick sing me their tales of over a century of previous tenants, but the whole time I was watching Em.

After a while she got up and took the painting of me off of the easel and leaned it against the wall. She put a fresh canvas in its place, and a shiver went through me as she picked up the small table and set up fresh jars of paint and cups of water. Then she made herself another drink and started working. As she worked, she kept making more drinks.

Anticipation grew inside me like a strange little creature as I watched, wondering what if anything would be done to me, would change me as she got deeper and deeper into the new piece. She started with a fiery red that covered the canvas, then pushed up yellows from the bottom like long leaves or flowers, then spent a good deal of time mixing together a watery violet that she added down the center, like a thin shadow in the flame.

Sometimes she leaned on the paint-splattered table, gritted her teeth and fought back sobs. If only I knew what was going on inside of her. If only I could better remember the time I was part of her, when we were one, but all I had was a room of water-damaged photographs – hazy images with emotions attached to them. Even the emotions – I had no way by which to sort them between positive and negative.

Em stomped away from the painting, yanking at her hair with her paint-splattered hands. She took a cup of watery paint and tossed it at the painting. She threw the canvas to the floor and kicked it across the room.

This whole time I felt nothing. Not so much as a feather twitched on my body. How could this be? How could I feel so empty while she suffers and feels so full? For the first time in my brief existence I felt disconnected from her – and worse, I felt like a voyeur up there watching her. I felt shame, like I had no right to be there. I felt separate from her.

Floating upward, I let myself pass through the ceiling and the small attic and up to the flat second-story roof. It had stopped raining, and the cool, moist air seeped into my feathers and skin and crawled down my throat when I breathed. I sat atop a quiet metal air conditioning unit, looking out at the neighborhood – at the shops across the street, the roofs of houses nearby, the large trees beyond in the parks singing their whispering praises to the clouds for the rain that was brought to them. Memories came to me of Em sitting there on that same air conditioner, or on the edge of the roof, looking up at the stars or out at the other buildings.

A fascination welled up inside of me – I was fixated on my lack of knowledge of Em's current condition. I had no idea if she was painting, crying or sleeping, or something else altogether. My lack of connection with her amazed me. Could I leave? What would happen if I wandered off – just went to another city? Would she get depressed or stop painting or die? Would I die? A chill went through me at the thought of her death. I felt the heaviness of my body on the air conditioner, felt the cool night air on my skin. I reached up and touched my own face. Was this face real? This body? Was this some sort of mask covering up something else? Not as important as my need for knowledge was my need to question – to see what I knew and didn't know. To touch the limits of my mind, if indeed it was a mind that I had.

I sat there for many hours. Listening to myself. Listening to the world. The sky had begun to lighten when I heard something and turned around. Em was standing there, across the roof, holding a bottle of water. Her face was flushed, her tired eyes looking right at me, seeing me.

"Mind if I join you?" she asked.

# chapter 9

I took a swig of water as above us the sky slowly morphed into morning. The convenience store's air conditioner sat as still as death underneath us. I was drunk and tired and my bones were sore. My eyes burned. But I felt good too. Sometimes it's good to cry and scream and throw things. Gets out the demons.

"So do you remember things?" I asked him. "I mean, do you have my memories?"

He shook his head. "Not really." His voice was so deep and smooth, like an open bass note. "There are images, pictures – but they hold no meaning. I am sorry, Em."

"Why?"

"As a part of you, I should be able to relate to you better, to better help you in times such as these."

"So you don't remember anything from before last night?"

"No. Nothing as clear as my memories of the last day's worth of time."

"I wish I could be like you. Clean slate, fresh start. That's why I moved halfway across the country. To get away from all the people who thought certain things of me. To get away from their eyes. To not have my memories staring me in the face every goddamn day." My eyes traced the rooftops, which began picking up the light as the sky slowly came to life. "You gonna fade away again?"

"I didn't fade away last night. You just couldn't see me or touch me. But I could see and hear you."

I closed my eyes and leaned my head on his shoulder, but he immediately twitched away from me. "That part of me is still sore."

"Oh. Oh yeah. Sorry about that."

He looked at me with those purple non-eyes. "I like the pain. It makes me feel like I'm real."

I reached up and touched his jaw. It was smooth and thick, but I couldn't tell if there was bone underneath or not. I ran my thumb over his lips, which were dry and cracked and dark. Black smoke fell continuously from his head in wisps like hair, down to his shoulders where it evaporated, and all I felt was cold air when I moved my hand through it. I reached into the shadowy smoke that wrapped around him like a cloak, and brought out his hand. It was the same pale violet as his face, the creases over his knuckles spidery and blue, his fingernails also dark blue. I held his hand in mine. "It's alright if you vanish again," I told him. "But if you do, you've got to come back."

He squeezed my hand very gently. "You seem... so fragile." He was looking down at my hand in his.

I laughed a little. "Don't tell anyone." He still seemed solid. I, on the other hand, was starting to lose my own solidity, and would have to find my bed soon. "Without digging too deep into my past, I must say that if you kill someone, I'm going to be really, really upset. If that happens, I'll have myself institutionalized – and you'll be really bored. So do me a favor, and just don't."

Those eyeless purple smudges looked deep into me. "Then I won't kill anyone. I don't think that I would have if you hadn't asked me not to, though."

I thought about saying, *That's the nicest thing anyone's ever said to me*, but didn't think he'd get the joke. I finished the rest of my water. "If there's any chance of me getting to work in ten hours, I'd better climb down to my bed." Then I handed him the empty plastic bottle. "Can you hold this?"

He took it from me. "I suppose I can."

"But you couldn't move things before, could you? When I couldn't see you?"

"I don't think so."

I hopped off the air conditioner and immediately the world twisted around me and pulled me forward. The ground came rushing towards me and then stopped. I was pulled backwards by W, who had a fistful of the back of my shirt. With his other arm he helped me stand and regain my balance, and when the world stopped spinning and I finished fighting off a bout of nausea I found myself leaning against his cool body.

"Are you alright, Em?"

"Yeah," I said. "Just forgot I was drunk and exhausted." I

found myself not wanting to move away from him. I didn't often find myself in someone's arms. And I guess I was alright with it since he wasn't really a someone. Then suddenly I felt really awkward and backed away. I looked up at him and had to squint to see if he was really fading away again. "It's happening again," I said.

"Then farewell," he said. "Though I am going nowhere. And have pleasant dreams, Em."

He began vanishing with the strengthening of the sunlight. I wrote that down on a mental note I hoped wouldn't get lost. "Try to move things," I said to him. "And try to speak to me."

"I will."

And then he was gone again. The same loneliness crept up inside me, but this time I didn't buy it completely – it crawled around inside my caverns like a strange goblin, but I knew W was still there, still standing between me and the air conditioner.

Carefully I made my way down the painted metal ladder and into my open window, plopping down onto my bed. Somewhere there were thoughts that floated above the surface like boats: *Did I set my alarm? I should take my shoes off. I should drink more water. Maybe I should close the window.* But they were so far off that I lost sight of them and fell into the sea.

*       *       *

I spent the early afternoon drinking lots of water and going back to bed, over and over again. Since taking on the life of the night/afternoon shift barista/artist, there were no longer weekends in my world; every night was Friday or Saturday night. The only difference between weekends and weekdays was whether the bars were packed or not, and that on weekends there tended to be more bands playing. I thought about this as I took two Advil – about not taking this life for granted, about enjoying this kind of cheap existence that gives me so much time to be creative. Sometimes at other coffee shops I see baristas who are sick of life, living one day to the next as if they loathe their existence, and there is an overwhelming urge inside to just punch them and scream at them to take themselves out of the mix and make room for someone who will appreciate such an unreal and beautiful way of living.

But I never punch them, give them advice, or even talk to them.

I just order, tip and leave, and remember not to become them – or
that if I *do* become them, it's time to change jobs.

I cleaned up the broken paint jars covering my floor. I'd have
to pick up some more paint thinner before cleaning up the paint.
Five thirty rolled around and I had a very quiet walk to work. The
sky was mostly clear, but it had been raining most of the morning
and the streets and sidewalks were still dotted with puddles, and in
the park I stuck to the walkways to avoid the mud. Inside The Cove
there were people at nearly every table but no one in line, and I
couldn't stop a smile from hijacking my face. I walked behind the
counter, dropped my bag, spun Red around and hugged her. She
hugged me back and picked me up off the ground.

"All the hoes are in the house!" she yelled.

"When did you get back?" I asked as she put me down.

"Few hours ago. Meesha was sick, and by sick I mean hung
over, and by hung over I mean her arms around the porcelain angel
puking her guts into its halo."

"You look good!" I said. "I thought you weren't coming back
for another couple weeks."

She pushed her thick, fire-engine-red dreadlocks away from her
face. She was one of the prettiest girls I'd ever met, half-Vietnamese
and half-Italian, and dressed like she lived in a post-apocalyptic
desert world. "Had to get out of Buffalo," she said, a little more
quietly. "Did a few art projects and the heat was on high. Thought it
was time to hide out back here in no-man's land. Don't know how
many times my credit card trick will work."

By this she meant the few times she had gone to jail and
received heavy fines for defacing private property, she paid off the
fines with a credit card and then filed for bankruptcy.

Red reached under a counter and pulled a folded up newspaper
out of her bag, then spread it out on the counter and pointed. There
was a picture of a three-story building with a logo of an eagle on its
sign, probably a credit card or loan company, and the building's face
was covered with splatters and spirals of paint. The caption under
the picture said: *Vandalism Or Art? Or Both?*

"Wow, it's huge," I whispered.

"Wait 'til you see the *color* pics. I'll probably develop them
tonight if you want to help."

"How did you do something this big? You couldn't have done
that with water balloons."

"No, did some paint balloon work while I was there, but not this building. One of the Buffalo group has been working on this contraption for years: it's essentially a giant squirt gun, kinda like a fire hose and kinda like a gattling gun, that shoots paint. He made it so that it comes completely apart, partially to clean and partially so that he can spread pieces of it all over Buffalo between projects."

"Seems a bit excessive."

Red shrugged. "He says this company here has put out hits on people before. But I think he's paranoid schizo." Her eyes widened. "But, hey, aren't we all?"

A few customers came up and we started helping them. I was so relieved that Red was back early – she was the best friend that I had. The *only* friend, really. At first I'd be afraid that she'd go to jail and not come out, or that she'd be shot by some confused security guard, but I'd eventually gotten over the fear, realizing that if she changed she wouldn't be *her* anymore.

"So, what's new here?" she asked when the customers had gone to a table with their drinks. "How've you been, Em?"

I bit my lip, thinking. "Crazy. Can I show you something at my house after work? It's a… painting."

"The way you say that makes it sound more like the Holy Grail." She tilted her head. "Em, did you paint something pornographic? Is this gonna make me sweaty?"

"Um… no."

She nodded to the door. "This guy ever ask you out?" The boyfriend guy was walking in.

"Nope."

She shook her head. "This city is so fucking boring!" she said as the guy walked up to me at the register.

I stared at him, waiting for him to speak first.

He nodded. "How's it going?" But behind the question seemed to be another, hidden question that should have been obvious to both of us - like at night we both met in some underground control room along with a few of the world's leaders and a few alien lords, and we all secretly control the fate of the universe, and the hidden question was, *How did you think the meeting went last night?*

I wore my best stone-face. "I'm doing well, thank you."

"Could I get a medium latte?" Another question layered behind it.

My hands clenched into fists and I had to pull one of them

open to ring him up. "It'll be three forty-five." At the espresso bar, Red started making his drink, somehow incorporating a great deal of pounding and slamming noises for such a simple drink.

He took out his wallet. "Usually it's three *eighty*-five."

"But that would be boring, wouldn't it?" I took his four one-dollar bills, gave him his change and shoved the register shut. "Other days belong to boring, not this one. This day says, 'Fuck boring.' Can't you hear it?" I turned and walked to the back counter before he could say anything, and started rearranging bags of coffee.

Red slammed his latte down on the counter. *"You ever gonna talk to her or are you just gonna stare at her all the fucking time?"* I kept rearranging coffee, glad he couldn't see me grinning. I surprised myself by feeling bad for him – no one who's so awkward and shy should have to cross paths with Red while she's fired up. Then Red was standing next to me, leaning back against the counter. "You know my horoscope says I'm only supposed to be having a two-star day? I feel like a fucking rock star."

"Have I ever told you I want to have your babies?"

She put a finger on her chin. "Never while sober... He's across the room, taking out his laptop. A bit shaken up, but don't worry, I don't think he'll be talking to you any time soon."

"It's been so boring without you."

"Do tell." She shrugged. "Or don't. Whatever's more entertaining. I totally trust your judgment in such matters."

chapter 10

While Em was working and talking to the girl with the red hair, I was attempting to alter the physical world - trying to slide coffee cups, to nudge straws that stuck out of people's glasses, and occasionally to whisper into Em's ear. I was crouched down next to a patron, trying to blow a napkin off of their table, when something pulled at my eyes from outside. There, in the evening sunlight, was a shimmering form – like a mirror bent into the shape of a person – who appeared to be standing upon an unoccupied table.

I stayed low as I flowed across the floor and peeked through the open doors. The slender figure lifted its arms up to the sky, as if in worship. Its back was to me. Then its arms lowered and I thought I saw it look down at the table it stood upon.

"There is no use hiding from me," said a bout of wind that brushed up against my ear. The voice invoked such a peace inside me – but even more so it hinted at some kind of vast, greater peace that was just out of reach, just over the horizon. It was a woman's voice, and the figure had the curves of a woman.

I stood up straight and floated outside, yet kept my distance. "I am called W," I said to her.

"You are newly incarnate." She turned and looked down at me. Her eyes were dual orbs of night sky, filled with black space and thousands of tiny stars. They were so deep that I felt I could reach into them, or get sucked inside and never return.

"Yes," I whispered. "I suppose I am."

Then she all but evaporated, except for the smallest sliver of movement, a rip in the air, which drifted down to the ground where she reformed in front of me. Her edges were uncertain, unclear – like only the blurry center of her had anything resembling solidity. The further out her form got from the center the more it lost its grip, until its edges gave up completely and merged with the wind. Even her hair, which was swatted about by wind I couldn't feel, was made up of blurred air. Only her star-filled eyes had any substance, though calling them substance didn't seem quite correct.

"Are you like me?" I asked.

"As alike as any of us are to each other." As she spoke, it seemed that her voice came from both sides of me, carried by winds from halfway around the world. "My name is Om." When she said her name, it was long and drawn out and utterly beautiful. Like she was describing all at once an artist's magnum opus and a secret, untouched pocket of rain forest and an incredibly simple monosyllable way to end every problem in the world. It was the most beautiful word I'd ever heard. Of course, I'd only heard less than two day's worth of words at that point, but I seemed to know every word that Em had ever known, and none were so powerful. But perhaps it was the way it was said that made it so.

"I must say," she said, "that you are very well-formed for such a young being. And your retainer is also very well-formed. You have done well."

"I didn't have much to do with it..." I glanced around at all the patrons sitting at tables, all quite unaware of our existence. "Would you like to go and sit at the fire pit?"

"Fire," whispered the air around me. I could see no trace of a mouth on her, nor any movement other than the squinting and widening of her eyes. "Just this once."

The fire pit was on the other side of the collection of war-broken buildings. It was made to look as though a building had been blasted apart, and the pieces of rubble were arranged into makeshift benches and laid out in a circle. In the center of the circle was a cluster of metal debris where a fire continuously burned. The area was currently empty, and I crouched on one of the brick and wood benches as Om floated nearby, staring at the fire.

"So, your... *retainer*... is in the coffee shop?" I asked.

"Yes. Yours is one of the workers? The dark haired one?"

"Yes, Em."

She turned to me then as her wind-voice spoke to me. "You must not elude yourself into believing that you do not completely exist, nor that you exist solely in the mind of your retainer. There are dangers for our kind, and you should not think that you are above harm. You should not trust so easily, as you are trusting me."

"What kind of danger?"

Om turned back to the fire, not answering. She stood between the fire and I, the red and orange flames dancing and twisting inside her form.

"You did not come from a painting," I said.

"No."

"Is your artist a glass-blower? Or perhaps a jeweler?"

She looked at me again with her eyes pulling at me. "Every day I am borne of sound. Every day I die in silence. Between the two I fly and thrive and breathe."

"Are you a part of that boy? The one with music on his computer?"

"Yes, but don't think that I came from that *machine*." She said the word *machine* with complete contempt. "Nor did I come from music. I am a note. A flawless pitch, quivering on the head of a pin. I am *Om*."

When her name rang out, the fire behind her flickered up and reached for the sky. Some people walking towards the parking lot glanced in our direction, but kept walking. She looked up and took a loud, deep breath, and the whole world around us seemed to relax. "It is almost the time of twilight, when the light of the sun and the moon mix like lovers in the sky. I must go now, and so should you, to your retainer – to teach and inspire them, to mold them into something great."

"Thank you for speaking to me, Om."

"Stay close to the girl, W." She blurred away to almost nothing and moved towards The Cove. I waited a few moments before following, and when I got there the boy was no longer sitting at his table.

# chapter 11

I was straightening chairs in the lobby, considering harassing the boyfriend guy when an alarm on his watch went off and he quickly packed up his laptop and left. Red was outside cleaning tables, and she glared at him as he walked by. I laughed, went to the back room to do some dishes and then I shrieked. My hand cupped over my mouth as I looked up at W floating there in the center of the back room like a gigantic feathered spider.

"You scared me!" I whispered.

"I'm glad you came back here," he said, "or I would have had to scare you out front. I had to know if you'd be able to see me right now."

Red ran into the back room, one of her hands in a fist with her index finger and thumb pointed out to make a mock-gun. She glanced around, but obviously couldn't see W.

"Sorry," I said. "Thought I saw... a walrus. I'm gonna take a break. Be back in five, alright? Or ten."

"A walrus?"

"Yeah, whiskers and giant teeth. Fat. Scary as hell."

Red scratched her temple with the barrel of the mock-gun. "Well, are you sure there aren't any outside?"

"I'm prepared now. I was just taken off guard."

Red put a hand on my shoulder. "You'd better take this." She handed me the mock-gun.

"What if walruses come into the shop? You'd be defenseless."

"I have coffee to throw on them. Besides, they'll have a lot of customers to eat through before they even get to me. I'll think of something."

I nodded and she pushed the mock-gun into my hand. My own hand became a gun and I slid it into the waist of my skirt, then walked out.

Red followed. "Everyone stay calm!" she said loudly to all the customers. "There are no walruses in the area! I've just confirmed it with the chief of security at the city zoo. False alarm – everything's fine. Please stay calmly seated between the entrance and myself."

I managed to keep a straight face as I walked out, W floating next to me. "So how did you know I'd be able to see you?" I asked as soon as we were away from The Cove and anyone who would hear us – or rather anyone who would hear *me*.

"Em, I think you can only see me at twilight."

I smacked my forehead. "I thought of that, last night when I was drunk." A group of people were walking through The Island. I took out my cell phone, pretending to talk into it as I looked into the windows of a trendy clothing store. "Did you just think of it?"

"I met another like me. Only she looked like a body of wind, with stars and night sky for eyes."

"Wow."

"She's part of that boy who sits in there. The one you don't like. Or do like."

My face dropped. "What? That weird guy? Was she as strange as him?"

"I'm not sure how beings like me usually act. Or how beings like you act. I didn't realize that the boy was strange."

"Hmm." I tongued my cheek. "This might *almost* explain why he's so weird. Did she come from a song of his?"

"She was very insistent that she came from *sound*, from a specific note."

Thoughts of the boy drifted through my mind, and in the reflection of the clothing store window W floated beside me. Shoppers looking through clothing racks in the store stepped into and out of his shadowy, feathered form. "Did she know? Did she know that you came from me?"

"She guessed it, but in the form of a question. So it seems she didn't know for sure."

I nodded. "Maybe he knew you were going to come from me, or maybe he thought you'd been around for a while. Could be why he looks at me the way he does. Maybe she told him."

My ear and cheek began buzzing and I jumped. I looked at my phone and there was a text message from Red:

AHHHH!!!!

"Gotta get back," I said, lowering my voice and rushing back to The Cove. "Try to move things on peoples' tables while it's still twilight. Let them think that it's ghosts or something."

I walked in and there was a line to the door, so I jumped behind the register.

\*          \*          \*

It stayed busy for a couple of hours, and near the end of the rush I was on the espresso bar and saw the boy come back. Seeing all the people in line, he went to one of the far tables and started setting up his laptop. I finished making everyone's drink, made a medium latte and walked over to his table and sat down. I set the drink down next to his laptop and he pulled off his headphones.

"How's Mrs. Wind?" I asked. *This is it*, I realized. *This is where I find out if I'm going crazy.* Like one of those movies where at the end you find out that everything was in the main character's head. Better than the ending where it's all a dream though – those are the worst.

He stared at me with those bright green eyes, his forehead draped in fallen curves of black hair that came to points like black claws. His corduroy jacket was on the back of his chair, and he wore a black T-shirt with a large white paw print on it. "My name's Matt."

"I'm so glad you said something. I thought I was going to punch you."

He nodded. "I don't always… interact well with people."

I tongued the inside of my cheek. "Do you *always* think of everything you're going to say before you say it?"

"Usually. I try to."

"That must be annoying."

"Not as annoying as what happens if I don't."

"Do you get slapped a lot or something?"

He shook his head. "I just don't make friends often. I don't relate well with other people."

"Maybe you just haven't met the right people. What about coworkers? Where do you work?"

"I design websites, so I pretty much work alone. People like my work and tell their friends about me, so I don't really have to go around selling myself or anything."

"Hmm. Ok. So, Matt, you knew I had a... an extension. Or that I was going to have one?"

He looked down at the keyboard, his eyes searching, then back at me. "I knew that you were like me, to some degree. Extension..." he said, his lips saying the word again silently. "What a great word for them. Like an extra limb, or an organ. Or software."

"Are there a lot of us around? People with extensions?"

"I don't know how many there are. I've met a few, seen maybe a dozen. Of course I don't know who's like us until my... extension tells me."

"How long have you had one?"

"A little over a year."

I tongued my cheek. "Do you play in front of people? Do you have a CD of your work?"

He seemed to sink down into his chair, his eyes pecking at the laptop keys. "I don't have any interest in an audience or money. My *extension* and I are all the audience we need. That's the beauty." He looked up at me with those green eyes. "That's the truth, the miracle of this life. We're different from other people, we live a different kind of life. We don't need them. We're self-sufficient."

"Hmm." I glanced around the room, at all the people engaged in their laptops or reading or talking. "I don't buy it." He was looking down at his laptop again. "It's like saying that 'cause you have a car there's no need to walk. Sure you don't have to interact with people, and maybe your wind-girlfriend keeps you from feeling too lonely, but you can't say that's what we're *meant* for. It's kinda like saying we're better than everyone else. And I don't think this happened to us so that we can feel superior." I reached over and picked up his latte and took a drink. "Maybe it's for each of us to decide what to do with it."

A pen on the table rolled off the edge and onto the floor. I smirked, wondering if it was W.

Matt powered off his laptop and took out his bag.

"We should work together," I said. "You can tell me what you know about all of this, and together we can figure out the rest."

"I've gotta go," he said, glancing over my shoulder. "Your co-worker needs you."

"Matt, you just got here. Did I say something mean? Was it the wind-girlfriend thing? Look, I'm sorry. I can be a bitch sometimes." I motioned around the shop. "Everyone knows. It's no secret."

He shoved his things into his bag and stood up. "I'll... I'll talk to you later, alright?"

I got up and followed him as he walked through the coffee shop, out the door and across the walkways of The Island. "Matt! Stop for a second. Please." When he didn't respond to me, I grabbed his shoulder and turned him around. "Why have you been coming here, staring at me all the time? Was this your plan? To tell me you're like me and then to run off and leave me to figure it all out for myself? To find someone like you and then go off and continue being alone?"

"You don't know anything about me."

"Except your biggest secret."

A howling gust of wind washed over us, making his hair scrape rapidly across his forehead, reaching down like a black-clawed hand to shield his eyes.

"I... I don't know what I was thinking. I don't know why I come here, or why I have an extension. I've got to go, and I'll talk to you later."

"You asked for me – every time you come in and look at me the way you do. You were *dying* for this conversation, and now you're running away from it."

He stepped away and turned his back to me.

"If you leave," I said, "don't bother coming back. You'll be eighty-sixed from The Cove. No one will serve you."

Matt just stood there with his back to me, not saying anything, his hand gripping the strap to his laptop bag.

A chorus of car alarms, maybe a dozen, erupted from the parking lot, a bird squawked overhead and a pack of giggling girls with pink shopping bags came out of one of the clothing stores. Something in the back of my head was whispering to me that I'd just made a step in the wrong direction. *Fuck off*, I said back to the voice.

Matt walked away. I threw my hands into the air and stalked back towards The Cove, the girls scattering like pigeons to make way for me.

Electronic noises and beats scurried across the cement floor of the coffee shop like little animals. I reached down to one of the beats and it rolled up my arm, onto my shoulder and pushed against the back of my head, nuzzling me like cat. The amorphous and shifting little creature, much like a pale ball of white smoke, rolled all the way down to my hand, and then back up to my shoulder. I began looking through all the hazy images of memory that I'd acquired from Em, and it occurred to me that perhaps people couldn't see sound. Not that I could see every sound, but little flurries of sound were constantly traveling about in packs, always in a constant state of diminishment.

It was then that I had a hypothesis. I looked over at the boy and Em sitting at the table and talking. I crept up close, took the flurry in my hand and nudged it towards the things on the table. It fell onto the table and rolled around, but the things on top remained undisturbed. I pushed my tongue, if you could call it a tongue, against the inside of my cheek while I thought. Then I tried blowing on the little sound creature. The flurry's form shimmered and vibrated and it tumbled forward, knocking a pen off the table.

I flew around to the other side of the table and picked it up. "I'm sorry," I said to the little creature. "I hope I didn't hurt you."

The flurry vibrated a little and began nuzzling against my arms.

"Good," I said. "I'd like to do it again if you don't mind."

The creature didn't seem to mind, though I wasn't sure that it understood me. I cupped it in my hands, brought it up between myself and the boy and blew. It hummed and vibrated in my hands and then shot out and froze in mid air, mere inches from the boy. The whole world before me was shivering and I realized that Om was standing directly in front of me, holding the flurry with one hand. She tossed it aside, grabbed me and yanked me up into the air, up through the ceiling and the attic and into the sky high above the coffee shop. The buildings of The Island and the neighborhoods all around became so small and miniature.

"I told you to trust no one!" howled the wind around me. "But it seems I was a fool to trust you!"

The wind ripped at the edges of me and her galaxy eyes made me lose all sense of direction, all sense of spacial relationship. I had to close my eyes to to keep my body from feeling like it was spinning. "I didn't think the vibration would hurt him!" I yelled over the wind.

"Don't pretend to be stupid with me anymore, W! What are you playing at? What's your real purpose here? What do you want with Matt?"

I was hurled downwards through the air and slammed into the cement ground of The Island's small parking lot. I felt cracks running through my body, cracks that made it more difficult to move. A shimmer above me caught my eye and I rolled away into the air as something slammed down next to me, black lightning spreading across the asphalt ground.

"Don't do this, Om! We are the same! We should not quarrel! I made a mistake!"

She glared at me with her galaxy eyes. "You and your retainer are a threat to me and mine."

"I would not hurt you, nor would I hurt him. I have no ill will towards you, and neither does Em. And she is no retainer of mine. She is more my soul, my life force, than anything resembling a 'retainer'. They are the bodies, we are the arms."

Om approached, her star eyes threatening to suck me up and swallow me, and I readied myself to move quickly. Then she backed away, heading towards The Cove. "Then I'll take some sound and blow it towards your precious Em. We'll see what it does to her."

I rose into the air, something like a heart pounding inside my chest. "I can't let you go near her, Om. You just attacked me."

"You'd be better off without her. You've let her blind you – let her confuse your purpose. I'll destroy her and you can form a new retainer, and perhaps you will keep a clearer mind." Then she lifted into the air and I followed, moving high above the cars and towards The Cove.

"Om!" I yelled out. My chest began to burn as I gained on her.

She flew down between the shops, where on the sidewalk Em and the boy were standing and speaking, and she was headed straight for Em. My feathers vibrated and pushed the world behind me as I dove down, colliding into Om and pulling her off course. We brushed right by Em, the wind from our bodies wafting over her and the boy. I held onto Om and pulled us high into the sky.

"Let me go!" roared the wind.

"No!" My skin seethed with rage, my chest seared with fire. "You will not touch Em! Never!" My organs churned and rearranged inside of me, the flesh of my chest singed with the heat inside, blackening and peeling back in flakes. Orange and red light broke through my chest in lines and patterns, and instantly I knew those symbols bursting from me – they were the symbols Em had drawn onto the refrigerator. As I realized this, the rage inside subsided completely, and on an even deeper level than before I felt that I knew what I was. I was W. I was Em's eyes for the other half of the world. I was her hands so that she could *hold* what she could not otherwise see or feel.

I looked down at the body of wind that writhed inside of my arms. "Om," I said quietly, "I will not hurt you, for you and I are the same. But I will not let you hurt Em."

She reached out and shoved her arm into the burning symbols on my chest, the wind of her ripping at the black smoke of myself. My breath caught, my head reeled backwards as lightning pain crackled through my body. The symbols tightened and seized her arm like chains, then quickly spiraled over her shoulder and around her torso. No thought could make itself heard inside my head as she and I roared out. I didn't know we were falling until just before we hit the cement of the parking lot, the impact creating a cacophony of vibration in the form of noise. Flurry-creatures of sound burst in waves from us, the little white animals colliding with the cars so hard that a chorus of car alarms arose into the air, spawning even more flurries.

I put a foot against Om's wind-filled, writhing form and pushed with all my strength, the symbols seeming to tear across her invisible flesh as I pulled them free of her and fell heaving and smoking to the ground, the symbols slowly slithering back to my body where they curled up against my chest. The world began to fade out, and I began a dialogue with it. "No," I said to it. "I have to make sure Em is safe."

"Look at the other one," the world around me said.

Glancing over at Om, I saw the last of her shivering body vanish.

I looked around at the noisy cars, at all the fluffy white balls of sound swirling about joyfully in the chorus of alarms, at all the people walking to and from their cars without a care in their eyes. "Who are you?" I whispered.

"That's not the question," said the world around me as it faded away, leaving me in utter blackness.

# chapter 13

"So... you've got this guy in your head that you can't usually see," said Red, "and he came from one of your paintings." We were meandering through a darkened area of the park, surrounded in every direction by a chorus of chirping cicadas and crickets.

"Yeah." I stepped over a tree root with only the parks' lights in the distance to see by. "That's the gist of it." *If I lose my best friend right now*, I thought, *I'll have to move away.* I wiped my palms on my skirt and clenched my teeth together to keep them from chattering, though it wasn't very cold at all. We walked up to the edge of the small pond and began walking around it's perimeter, towards a herd of ducks who had their heads buried under their wings, sleeping.

"Well, the guy in your head sounds a lot more interesting than the laptop guy." Red took a puff off her cigar and blew a few smoke rings, the breeze ripping them to bits only a few inches from her lips. I loved the smell, it always reminded me of her. "But if this W fellow ever tells you to start burning shit, you come see me right away, is that clear?"

"Clear as vodka."

"'Cause he probably doesn't know half as much about burning shit as I do. I could save the both of you a lot of time." She stopped walking and stepped towards me, her red mane falling forward around her face. "Are you crying, Em?"

"Sorry." I wiped one of my eyes. "Just thought... you might not..."

She smiled. "You thought I'd think you were crazy."

"Something like that."

She put a hand on my shoulder. "You *are* crazy, Em. I don't talk to sane people. And I especially do not do shots with them, or

share my artwork with them, or tell them where I sleep at night."
She tilted her head. "Doesn't mean I don't believe you really have a
painting-apparition following you around. But you *are* nuts."

"Thanks," I sniffed. "Makes me feel all warm and fuzzy
inside."

She pulled me into a hug. More tension than I ever thought my
body could hold suddenly released and Red had to balance the both
of us as I went completely limp in her arms.

"You're gonna be alright," she whispered. "You've got me." I'd
rarely heard Red sound so serious, and I hugged her back, my hands
making fists with the back of her shirt, my head buried in the spot
where her neck met her shoulder. "And anyway, you're kind of a
badass, girl. Most people don't have the courage to just move across
the country by themselves. Start up fresh. Especially after what
you've been through."

I clenched my eyes shut. "You're all I have."

She put a hand on my head and held me there, in the park under
the clouds and the stars.

*            *            *

The door jingled as we walked into the convenience store. Abid
was behind the counter reading the newspaper.

"Abid? What're you doing working the graveyard?" I asked
him, my voice still hoarse.

"Had to let someone go." The skin around his eyes was
sagging, and he looked dead tired. He glanced at my feet. "You must
have found a poor child to steal shoes from. This is good. You are
free to come in and spend money."

"Thanks." I walked around the small store, but there was
nothing there I needed. I felt much better, and just wanted to get Red
upstairs so she could see the painting.

Red leaned onto the counter, smirking up at Abid. "Hey cute-
stuff, can I get that bottle of Jameson?" It had taken us a few months
to realize that Abid was awkward when Red was around because he
had a crush on her. He never hit on her or anything – as far as I
knew he never hit on anyone. But Red liked to make him blush
every chance she got.

"Yes, Miss." He grabbed the bottle from the rack behind him
and set it on the counter. "Is that all? You need Pepsi or anything?"

"Pepsi..." Red whispered the word, as if it were a foreign concept. "You mean to mix? And completely destroy the delicate balance of this precious Irish whiskey?" Then she leaned even closer. "*Pussies* mix alcohol, Abid. Do I *look* like a pussy?"

His cheeks turned crimson. Red set some bills onto the counter and unscrewed the cap from the bottle. Abid pressed buttons on the register and took the cash, and Red took a swig. She licked her lips and offered him the bottle. "Want to see what my lips always taste like?"

"Not... not on the job."

Even in my weird state I had to smirk. When we walked outside and I was unlocking the door to the stairwell, Red was laughing. "What's with guys having crushes on us and not doing anything about it? Seems like they're all the same. Think Abid there's got one of them art-spirits following him around too?"

"I think he would have told me if he was an artist, or a musician or whatever. Maybe you should try getting to know him better. When it's just me and him, he's sarcastic as hell, and really funny. I think the two of you would hit it off."

"Yeah, maybe. I just get bored with people too easily, and just end up telling them they're boring and offending them."

"I'm boring, and you hang out with me."

"You, my dear, are not boring."

We started walking up the stairs.

"Also," said Red, "I can't figure out if I'm in the mood to date girls or guys right now. Girls have the interesting and complicated parts down, but are more trouble than they're worth half the time. And guys are either boring, using you, or both." She elbowed me. "If I could time travel to before we became friends, I'd just date you. That'd be easy. Well, except for the time traveling part."

"Yeah, like I'm not more trouble than I'm worth."

Red shrugged as I opened the door to my apartment. "You're the only person worth dating in this city. Too bad you're like my sister – otherwise, there'd be no holding back. Some people are into the whole sister thing, but not me."

"You'll find someone." I turned on the light. "Or they'll find you."

"You know, that thing you did on the refrigerator at work – it looks cool and all, but I didn't think much of it at first. Then for my whole shift I just couldn't stop staring at it. It's... it's good. The lines are really nice."

"Thanks," I said, walking over to pick up the easel I'd kicked earlier.

"There's glass on the floor."

"Yeah, you might not want to take your shoes off." I picked up the painting of W, took a deep breath, and put it on the easel right-side-up, or at least the way I painted it.

"Jesus, Em..." Red whispered. She immediately walked up to it, standing there with her hands at her side, staring at it.

I walked over to where she'd set down the Jameson, picked it up and took a swig, trying not to cough but failing. I really wasn't a whiskey girl. Closing my eyes, I tried to feel W, imagining him behind me with his arms wrapped around me. My heart was pounding loud but not too fast, the heaviness of the bottle pulling my hand towards the floor, the whiskey tingling on the surface of my lips. I opened my eyes, walked over to a clear spot on the floor and sat down with my back against the wall. I took a few more sips from the bottle, and Red just stood there staring at the painting.

After a long time, Red spoke, slowly. "I feel like my insides are spinning when I look into this. I can't even think clearly." She looked at me. "No one else has seen this?"

I shook my head.

"Don't sell it," she said. "We'll force Jacob to let us put it up in The Cove. Or put it up somewhere. People are gonna flip out over this."

I handed her the bottle of Jameson and she took a long drink.

"Now go over there and flip it upside down," I said.

She looked over her shoulder. "I'd rather not. I don't really want to touch it."

"Red," I said, giving her a stern look. "Take another swig, grow some balls and go flip it."

"Yes ma'am." She took a drink, handed the bottle back to me and walked over. She turned it upside down very carefully, then took a few steps back. "Hmm."

"Can you see him?" I asked.

"Who? You're invisible friend?"

"Yeah, he's in there."

She moved very close to it. "Holy shit! That's his face?"

"Yeah."

"Creepy little devil. So you painted him first?"

"I painted it right-side up, pretty much completely wasted. Then I found him in my apartment when I got home from work, even attacked him with a bottle thinking he was a burglar, and he told me that it was upside down because of how the eyes and brain flip things. He also said that I named him W, because of the W there in the corner, even though I meant it as an M."

"Em, whatever you have to do to keep him..." she shook her head, still staring at the face in the painting. "I'll bring him grapes and wine and fan him while wearing skimpy clothing if you keep painting things like this."

"I'll be sure to let him know how you feel."

She stepped back, tilting her head from one side to the other. "You need to show both viewpoints. What you need is a mirror." She nodded, turning the painting right-side-up again. "An angled mirror so that both effects of the piece can be seen. I can build you one."

"I don't know if that would fit at The Cove. A mirror just sticking out of the wall like that?"

"Screw The Cove. We'll make it fit. Throw a table out if we have to. Jacob will understand, especially once he sees this."

I got up and walked over. "A mirror..." I really liked the idea.

"I'll try to come up with something within the week. Can't promise, though. Not sure if I have enough scrap metal lying around – we might have to go dumpster-diving. Maybe we could hang it up without the mirror first."

"No. We should wait until we have the mirror. Don't want to half-ass it."

"Cool. Look, I should get home and unpack, not to mention start developing some of my film. You gonna be alright, girl?"

"I will be now, thanks to you."

"You need anything, just give me a ring."

"Will do."

She smiled and I threw my arms around her and hugged her tightly.

"I could stay for a while," she said.

"No, I'm alright now." I kissed her forehead and bid her farewell.

After Red left, I swept up the broken glass and began to tidy up.

chapter 14

Once again I came back to consciousness lying on the ceiling of Em's room. She'd obviously cleaned it up from the night before, and she was down below me wrapped in sheets, eyes closed and breathing softly.

My mind drifted to those words of the world in the parking lot. What did it mean by, "That's not the question"?

I tried to move, but my chest felt like an open wound.

Below me, Em muttered my name. "W. Lay down next to me." I could not tell if she was awake or dreaming. I floated down to lay behind her. "Put your arm around me." I did as she asked, wincing, and kept my chest from pressing against her back. Her hair smelled of coffee and chocolate and sweat. I closed my eyes and felt her breathe, the sheets almost nothing between us. Her hand pressed up against mine, and I felt it, though I knew that it was not going to be twilight for quite some time.

The bed began to pull me into it, and my closed eyes began sealing themselves shut. My breathing slowed, syncing up with hers, and my body fell apart and spun away from me. I was left alone in a darkness that was deep and spacious and empty, and I floated inside of it for quite some time.

Then a light came from behind me, washed over me, and I was suddenly standing in the middle of a wheat field. The wind pulled gently at the edges of my body, and I could see yellow rolling hills and clusters of trees and dirt roads and fences for miles around, all underneath a milky blue sky. *This is the town where Em grew up*, I realized. *But the buildings and the houses have gone underground.*

The yellow wheat brushed against my legs.

"You've come full circle," said a small voice.

I turned to see a crow perched upon a short, skeletal tree, eye-level with me.

"I've never been here before," I said. "Not really."

The crow flapped its wings. Its beak opened and closed. "Its good to have my feathers back. Since she gave them to you, I haven't been able to fly. I missed the sky."

Looking down at my body, I saw that indeed my feathers were not there. I felt naked without them, and folded my arms over my chest, which wasn't as sore. I moved to lift up into the air, and nothing happened, as if my body had such an incredible weight, or as if my feet were tethered to the soil.

"What's happened to me?" I asked the crow. "And what happened to this town?"

"Her friends always called her scarecrow, back where she's from."

"I know that." I could almost see the faces of her old friends, but the images were too hazy to make out.

"There it is!" whispered the crow. "Don't let it hurt me again!"

I turned and there was a scarecrow sitting cross-legged upon a small boulder, neither of which had been there a moment ago. Its clothing was made of burlap, it wore a long-brimmed hat and had branches for arms and hands. "Back home," said the scarecrow, "they called me scarecrow. Because of my clothes, and because of how thin I was." Then I realized that the scarecrow was Em. Her hair fell all the way down to her shoulders and there were dead leaves and long grass woven all through it. "How do you feel about feathers?"

I licked my lips, which felt cold and dry. "I enjoy not being confined to the ground, but I do not wish others to suffer for my sake."

The scarecrow looked disappointed. She glanced down at both of her tree-branch hands. "You are so much better equipped than I am."

The wind picked up around us. I could feel the crow's fear as it stood on the tree behind me, ready to take flight if the scarecrow were to make any sudden moves.

"Everything in this world falls away," said the scarecrow. "Eventually."

Then the wind swirled around us so loud and strong that it lifted her away like she was made of paper.

"Em!" I screamed. Instinctively I tried to lift into the air and fly after her, but fell onto my side.

"Difficult not to have wings," said the crow.

I got up and followed Em with my eyes as she got smaller and smaller so far above me.

"I had to climb and hop when I couldn't fly," the crow said. "And I looked ridiculous." I turned and the tree the crow perched upon was now thicker and reached far up into the sky, like a twisted brown spine with branches sprouting from it. The crow flew backwards and up into the air just before the bark-skin of the tree burst into flames, the fire quickly rolling up the tree in waves. The tree reached far into the sky until it disappeared, close to where Em was just a tiny dot.

I leaped onto the tree and began climbing furiously, the heat of the bark tearing at my palms and at the souls of my feet. The fire wafted over me as I pulled myself higher and higher, but my body did not catch. Looking up, I could barely see the dot of Em through the orange flames. My whole body ached from the heat, and my insides felt as dry as desert. The bark was breaking beneath my grip, slipping from the tree's body.

"Thirst," said a voice behind me. I turned and the crow was there flapping its wings. "If you ever want to become a real boy, you have to recognize these things."

I hugged the tree to keep from falling, though the pain this caused my body was astounding. "I have nothing to drink."

"What's that bulge in your coat?"

I looked down and indeed I was wearing a coat, and I reached inside of it, finding an inner pocket and pulling out a brown bottle. I wanted to consume what was inside of it more than I'd ever wanted anything. Immediately I poured the liquid down my throat, and the liquid burned but also quenched my thirst. When the bottle was empty I licked at the open neck of it, and then I saw the fire crawl quickly up the sides of the bottle, tracing the spilled liquid across the surface and then inside. The bottle exploded in my hand, shards of glass falling down into the vast space below me, then the fire crawled up the liquid that had spilled all over the front of me in my sloppy consumption. Quickly I tried to wipe the liquid from my lips and chin, but the fire was over my hand and quickly burst into my mouth and down my throat.

The roaring sound of the fire stopped, as did all sound, and all I heard was distant screaming, though the screaming did not sound like me. My arms and legs unwrapped themselves from the branches. I looked down at my hands and arms as my skin split open in long, yellow slits, and I had to squint against the light pouring from the slits, light that was growing rapidly inside of me, growing larger than my body and breaking through me like I was a just a shell. My skin ripped and peeled quickly away in long strips, and I was falling backwards. Above me the very sky broke open in the same way, peeling back in a brilliant array of yellows and oranges that seared into my eyes.

Then the sky itself reached down with flowing yellow and orange hands and caught me, pushing me back against the ground or a wall. I was blinded by the tempest of light, and in it I could make out Em's face, which was completely made of yellows and oranges and looked to be consumed in rage.

"If something happens to her, I'll kill you!" she screamed. "Why aren't you with him right now?" She pointed behind her, and slowly the oranges and yellows behind her began to resemble her room. She was standing and holding me against a wall.

"Em," I said. "I'm not sure what you..."

"You should be there for him! I should be there for him! What if he gets lost?" She slid to the ground, pulling me down with her, and leaned forward against me. The light coming from her body vibrated and buzzed against my skin. I held her in my arms and stroked her hair. "What if he gets lost in there and I never see him again?" she sobbed.

"Everything going to be alright," I whispered to her.

"I've never had you," she cried. "I've never had you."

She sobbed against me, and the sobs turned to heavy breathing, and she grew calmer until I was sure that she was asleep. She slid down me and curled up on the floor. I flew over to the window, which she must have opened, and tried to close it with no success. I looked around at the dark room, with all the light radiating from Em's body doing nothing to lighten the room, and decided to go up to the roof for some fresh air, and to ponder.

# chapter 15

I sat cross-legged on the pale sofa, wearing my blue pajamas with yellow bananas printed on them, a blanket half-wrapped around me. My hair was pulled back into a pony tail. Everything in the living room was white, or something close to it – my mom always liked things to look pure. There were mirrored tiles behind the entertainment center, and the TV was on. There wasn't any volume coming from the TV, but I could understand what the cartoon characters were saying by reading their body language and their lips.

The clanking of dishes and pots came from the kitchen as my dad made breakfast. Sunday was always our day – while mom went to church, me and dad would have breakfast, then we'd always do something like go to one of the creeks, or explore abandoned buildings outside of town, or go to a coffee shop and make up articles based on the headlines in the newspaper until everyone was staring at us because we were laughing so hard. I never understood why he was with my mom – he always seemed so much cooler than her. It's like she'd just given up on life a long time ago and decided to live the American stereotype rather than be what she wanted to be back when she used to have desires. My dad never seemed to mind that his wife had become a church-going housewife who bakes (rather poorly), smiles more than she really wants to and is completely content for everything to stay exactly the same until she dies of old age.

I turned around on the sofa, pulled open the off-white curtains of the large window behind me and looked out into the neighborhood. The sky was white with morning clouds. The houses were thin and tall, and most had pillars leading from the front porches up to the second floors. All had perfectly manicured lawns, and all were white or off-white, except for one house that was almost directly across the street. It was only one story, and was a deep red with a jet-black roof. There didn't seem to be any curtains on the windows, but the windows were pitch black, like two square, black eyes watching all that went on in the neighborhood. The red porch had a single black rocking chair standing sentinel next to the door.

"Hey dad," I said. "Who lives in that red house? I forget."

My dad walked into the living room. He was clean-shaven and had on a green sweater. He leaned over the couch and looked out the window with me. "Oh, that place? It's what they call *front of house*. No one really lives there. Inside there are doorways to other peoples' souls." He laughed. I always loved his laugh – it was as if he found everything to be completely absurd. "The neighborhood hates it because it's in the city guidelines that they can't paint it or anything. Have to just let it be."

"That's comforting. At least there's something they can't beat down into utter normalcy."

"There's someone going in," he whispered.

A man got out of a car that had pulled up in front of the house.

"Looks like you," I said. "That's weird."

"Yeah."

The man who looked like my dad had a day or two's worth of stubble on his face and was wearing a long, brown trench coat. He walked around and opened the passenger door and a girl about thirteen got out – a girl with long red hair and a black T-shirt. The wind picked up outside and the trench coat lifted behind the man like a cape, and the girl's hair blew about wildly.

"That's... that's my friend Red," I realized. "I haven't met her yet, but she becomes my friend when I move away. I should go and say hi."

"You can't go out there," said my mom. I turned and it was my mom instead of my dad who was leaning forward looking out the window. Her face looked calm and she wasn't smiling.

"You're supposed to be at church," I said.

"I'm not feeling well, so I didn't go. Besides, you need your breakfast."

"How come dad's hanging out with someone else?" I said, raising my voice. "You're not supposed to be here. I should be the one out there with him, not Red."

I got up and walked to the door.

"It's locked," said my mom, still looking out the window. "You can't go out there right now. You don't want to be with him. Just wait a while. Watch your cartoons."

I went to the window and saw them walking across the lawn towards the house. "Dad! I'm in here! Red!" I struggled to open the window. "What are they doing? Why are they going in there?"

"I have blueberries for your pancakes," said my mom.

"I don't fucking care!" I unlatched the window and pulled it open. The wind that rushed into the living room was cold.

My mom grabbed me up from behind and pulled me away from the window. "Em! You *can't* go out there!"

"You're not even supposed to be here! You ruin everything!"

Across the street, my dad opened the door and young Red went inside. He glanced around the street to see if anyone was watching.

I shook my head, tears flowing down my face, still being held back by my mom's arms. "What's he doing?" I screamed. "If something happens to Red, I'll fucking lose it in the future! She's the only friend I have when I move away!"

"Why would you ever move away?" asked my mom.

My dad stepped inside and shut the door, and I screamed.

My mom let me go. "You can go out there now. But put a coat on. It's chillier than it looks."

I spun around and shoved her up against the entertainment center, grabbing fistfuls of her dress in my hands. The edges of her blurred from my tears. "If something happens to her, I'll kill you! Why aren't you with him right now?" I pointed to the window. "You should be there for him! I should be there for him! What if he gets lost?" My knees grew week and I slid to the ground, pulling her slowly down with me. I leaned my head against her shoulder. "What if he gets lost in there and I never see him again."

"You still have me," said my mom.

I shook my head. "I've never had you," I whispered as I closed my eyes. "I've never had you."

*     *     *

When I woke I was curled up in a ball on my floor with some dirty clothes pulled around my feet. The window was open and cold air lapped at my face. I went to the bathroom, drank some water and looked at myself in the mirror. My face was pink from crying, and I looked terrible. I hadn't had one of those dreams for a few months. I had hoped I was done with them.

The sky was beginning to lighten and I didn't see W anywhere, so I threw on some clothes and a jacket and climbed up to the roof, where I found him sitting on top of the air conditioner.

"Sorry if I said anything out loud," I said. "I have these dreams from time to time."

"It's alright. I had a sort of dream as well."

"What about?" I climbed up and sat next to him. I massaged one of my arms which was sore from lying on my floor.

W seemed sad, or pensive. "You were a scarecrow, and the wind swept you away and I couldn't fly so I climbed a tall, burning tree to try to get to you. There was a crow as well who talked to me, said he'd taken his feathers back, which is why I was affected by gravity."

"Sounds pretty heroic." I crossed my legs underneath me. "I dreamed about my dad. You don't remember any of that, right?"

"Nothing."

I took a deep breath.

"Em, you don't have to tell me. I don't really understand memories anyway."

"I want to tell you, W. I mean, you're kind of stuck with me, so it wouldn't be fair for you not to know. Also, I haven't told anyone for a while. And I think it would feel good, in a way."

He looked at me with his black non-eyes and his blue lips. "Then I'd wish to hear it."

I shivered a little and took a deep breath. Red was the only person I'd told for years, though I wasn't sure that W counted as a *person*. "My dad and I always got along. I always felt like I was the friend my dad wanted when he'd married my mom. She must have been really cool at some point for him to want to marry her. Even when I went through rebellious phases, they were mostly against my mom, who I'd started to think wasn't even a real person. He'd drive me and my friends to concerts, pretend to like our music and always slip me some money when mom wasn't looking." I laughed weakly. "This probably doesn't mean anything to you."

"It is important to me. To know you is to know myself."

I swallowed, my throat feeling raw inside. "Alright. When I was fifteen, the cops broke down our door with their guns out and arrested him. They'd surrounded the house. There were even helicopters." I began to shake, my teeth chattering and my voice breaking as I spoke. "It turns out that for years he'd been kidnapping young girls, doing horrible things to them, burying their bodies in some abandoned barn outside of town." My face grew warm with tears as images flooded through my mind of newspapers and court rooms. "The newspaper had sketches of him in court – just sitting there... staring at the table. Broken. He was the only person I've ever loved. And the only person who's ever loved me. Now he lives in a prison on the other side of the country."

"Do you still love him?"

"What the hell is that supposed to mean?"

"I thought... You said he was the only person you..."

"I *know* what I said, W." I leaned forward, staring down at the cracked and peeling rooftop below my feet. "I don't know. I don't know how I feel about him."

"Em," he said.

When I looked up at him, he was fading away. "Red loves you."

And then he was gone.

"I know," I whispered. I knew that what he said would make me feel better in a day or so, but at that moment it didn't seem to matter at all.

chapter 16

Floating high above Em's apartment, I was like a cloud of gas. The sun's light pulled at my edges, stretching them out like thin black and blue teeth. I felt the warmth, knew the warmth, yet there was nothing in me to retain any of it. The only things that left lasting impressions upon me, as far as I could tell, were knowledge, especially of a self-discovering nature, and the transformations which occurred when I and Em were linked – when we would meet halfway between our respective dimensions, and the impressions we had upon each other were vast and full of potential.

Was there some higher reason for these "meetings" that we had? I couldn't help but to see meaning in everything – in the way she tied her shoes in the morning, in the way she became like a child as she slept, in the way she used her hand on the inside of the bathroom sink to wash the toothpaste away. Yet I had no idea *what* any of it meant, just that everything was so completely sacred. I felt the whole world opening up with so many tiny molecular bursts – every wall, every door and tree and rock and bird was a conglomeration of millions of tiny openings, tiny eyes, all of them looking back at me with the same overwhelming curiosity with which I'd come to look at them.

Though standing like a monolithic pyramid covered in writing that I could not comprehend, with a history that eluded me and a future of so many incomprehensible roads, was Em. For I knew I was connected to her on levels I did not yet understand, and she was connected to this sacred world in ways that I could not imagine myself ever being connected to it. She was my gateway into the vastness that surrounded us. I was almost completely certain that when she ceased to exist in her body, the molecules that made up myself and this form would disperse, and I would become a different aspect of this sacred world.

After a long while I felt a stirring within me, a tickle like a small insect walking across my insides. I turned around in the sky and let myself fall slowly down to the roof and through it into Em's apartment. Her bed was empty and I could hear the shower running. It shut off and soon Em walked out wrapped in a towel. The edges of my body, still malleable and lengthened by the sun, reached out across the walls like black and blue ivy, growing longer and braiding into each other, until they all but covered one entire wall of her small apartment. I watched her grind coffee and put water on to boil. If anyone watched her as intently as I watched her, I would consider them a threat and protect her from them.

She began humming to herself and the tiny, white, cotton-ball flurries that came from her closed lips spiraled down around her body and circled around her feet on the concrete floor. The walls, floor and ceiling, as well as the wood and brick underneath, all had come to love her in their way. They'd seen so many tenants come and go, and would surely see many more, but they claimed to me that they would remember Em in ways they would remember no one else. I was not sure whether or not brick and wood could embellish the truth or just outright lie, but I decided to believe them.

As I lay there wrapped up in myself and covering the wall, an energy gathered inside of me. Subtle yet strong, it built itself up, feeding itself until I began shaking against the wall, my eyes absorbing everything in the room. This energy was a sort of pure potential, yearning to go nowhere and everywhere at the same time.

Then there was movement. My edges dislodged from the wall and I floated forward in space, the rest of me trailing behind like flat tentacles. Em was standing there by the stove, a cup of coffee in her hands, sipping it. My body must have taken up most of the apartment with all of me stretched out so thin. I reached down and cupped her face in my hands, a jewel which defined all laws of time, a jewel which was hidden in front of all, and I lifted her face up to mine. Our eyes locked and I reached down, took her coffee cup and set it on the counter.

I crawled onto her, wrapping my legs around her toweled body with her face in my hands. Her head tilted back as her lips parted. My mouth found hers, and I said her name into her mouth, the end of the word becoming a resounding hum that traveled through her lips, across her cheeks, down her chin and neck and up her forehead.

Then her lips moved and she said my name against my own lips. The symbols inside my chest stirred to life, the whole world shattering and exploding into orange and yellow light, like the previous night. I was propelled slowly backwards into the room. She was glowing and burning, staring up at me, fire within fire within fire, as the whole room burst around her with fiery light.

She looked down at her hands, and I found myself compelled to float to the painting of me. It was the only thing in the room that held any darkness, the violets and blues swirling slowly on its surface. I took the painting down from the easel and replaced it with the painting she'd been working on, the one she'd doused with water and paint.

The floor rippled at her steps as she walked towards the painting. I dragged the table of paints up to the easel and opened the jars. When she dipped her fingers into one of them, there was a resounding *boom*, as if a building across the street had been lifted high into the sky and then dropped. She lifted her hand to the painting.

*Boom.* It was closer now. Louder.

She touched the canvas.

*Boom.* My chest ripped up the center, and a storm of implications dawned on me as light spilled out from inside my body. I would forever be changed here, in this place. Like a random pattern drawn by wind in the sand, I could be rearranged, made into anything. And here, this place, was where Em becomes the wind.

Here, this place, is where I die.

Tears of light dripped down my face.

Her hand traveled over the length of the canvas.

*Boom.* I clenched my teeth as my chest peeled open. "I trust you, Em," I cried as my molecules flipped like coins, one at a time becoming something other than what they'd been. All my memories, my feelings, were being ripped away from me. "I love you, Em. Goodbye."

*Boom.*

This place, this is where I die, and this is where I was and will be born.

# chapter 17

Adrenalin was still coursing through me from painting all day and I nearly missed my stop on the bus. I'd felt the inspiration dwindling and had made myself stop painting so I wouldn't ruin it. I don't know what W did, but I was gonna have to tell him to do it again tomorrow. I was even considering calling out of work tomorrow to work on the painting.

I walked the few blocks from the bus stop down the crooked sidewalks and broken streets towards Red's place, past boarded-up houses, cars rattling from the bass booming inside them, and people enjoying the afternoon sunlight on their front porches.

"Hey pretty girl!" yelled a bearded, smiling black man hanging out with some people on his front steps. "You goin' to see Miss Red?"

"Maybe I just came by to see *you*, Duke."

"'Course, girl! Everyone's really commin' here to see The Duke, even if they don't know it. Hey, I got somethin' for you." He got up and ran into the house.

I said hi to the other three men, who all seemed to have a nice after-work buzz going on.

The Duke walked out with two tall Miller High Lifes. "For you an' the Miss," he said and gave them to me.

"Awe, thanks Duke." I slipped the cans of beer into my bag.

"Ain't nothin'. Hey, if you're walkin' back after dark, you come by this way an holler if no one's out here. Me or one of these courtly gentlemen will see you to safety. You don't want to be wanderin' around these parts at night."

"Sure thing. Have a lovely evening, gentlemen." I curtsied to them with my quilted skirt and continued down the street.

Red lived in a large brick factory that had been gutted and

sectioned off into rooms. The rent was cheap and the landlord only rented rooms to artists and musicians. They lacked insulation, heat and a kitchen, but, as Red liked to say, "They had an abundance of soul."

I unlocked the main door with the key she'd given me and went inside, up the rotted-out wooden stairs and through a room full of stage props and giant paintings, past several old doors and up to her door, which was painted red with a giant black X on it with the word CONDEMNED stenciled underneath. The soothing, steady beats of triphop music were lazily and loudly pouring from behind the door, so rather than knock I unlocked it and went inside.

Her room was much larger than mine, and she'd built a wall in the center and knocked down the walls of the bathroom so that the window-less half of her room served both as her bathroom and as a dark room to develop her photographs. In it she had shelves of chemicals and tables with trays on them, and also used her bathtub for part of the process. The front room consisted of a beat-up but super-comfortable red couch, a stereo system with several large speakers, a rack of pans and plates and a hot plate, and a short table covered in cut up magazines and newspapers with an exacto blade sitting on top. Her dresser was in the photo lab/bathroom, because she didn't want to know what she was putting on when she was getting dressed. Her room, as always, smelled of chemicals from the developing process.

She wasn't in the front room, so I threw the High Lifes into the dorm fridge, then plopped down on the couch, picked up a magazine about anarchy and skimmed through the articles. Eventually Red walked out of the thick, black-curtained doorway with her bug-like World War I gas mask strapped over her face. She tried to talk but her voice was all garbled and drowned in the beats of the music. She pulled the mask up and onto her dreadlocks. "Hey girl! That time already?"

I shrugged. "I don't check the time on my days off. I'm probably early."

She walked up, tilted her head and stared into my eyes. "What's going on in there?" She tapped my forehead.

"I had a dream about my dad last night. And I started a new painting today."

"Sounds like a productive twenty-four hours. Or less than twenty-four hours. You alright?"

"Yeah, just a bit stirred up."

"The house across the street again?"

"Yeah, but this time he was taking *you* into the house – you as a little girl. And I knew that if he killed you I wouldn't end up being friends with you."

"Wow, that's some heavy shit. You sure you're ok?"

"As ok as I ever am."

Red walked over and opened the window. "You want a drink?"

"There are a couple High Lifes in the fridge, complements of The Duke."

"Bless that man's soul."

"I'm not up for a beer yet," I said as she grabbed one and opened it.

Red took a swig and sat down on the table, facing me. "You give any more thought to contacting your dad?"

I shivered and hoped she didn't notice. "Every so often, but my stomach knots up when I think about it. And I've really gotten to like my life here, just the way it is." I leaned forward on the couch, looking down at the backs of my hands. "I can't think of anything he could say that would change a fucking thing. Maybe I would feel different, but I wouldn't feel any better."

"One thing to keep in mind is the Em in the future. You know how you feel now, but things change and feelings change. He's going to die in prison, and he's probably going to die before you do."

I looked up into Red's eyes.

"There's a window of time," she said, "in which you can decide whether or not to talk to your father. Only you don't know how long that window will *stay* open. My advice is for you to decide while the window is open, because if it closes before you've made up your mind you'll never know whether you wanted to talk to him or not. You might tell yourself that you wanted to or didn't want to, but you'll always be uncertain inside of what you should have done."

I reached out and touched her hand. Red's father left her mother when she was a little girl, then when Red was a teenager he died of a heroin overdose. "All we have," she said, "are our passions and our opportunities. And our only real enemy is time." She smirked. "Though don't tell time I said that, I like to let it think we're friends. It's all about sleeping with the enemy."

I squeezed her hand. "Want to share a smoke?"

"Hell yes."

We climbed out the window and onto the fire escape, where Red had a few small plants. Sitting on the metal stairs, we shared a cigar and the second can of High Life as the sun fell behind a curtain of white clouds and towards the horizon.

"Man," said Red, "being around those chemicals all day really makes you appreciate what real air smells like."

"She says as we sit here smoking a cigar."

"Hey, this smoke's more real than that shit." She pointed into her apartment with her thumb.

"Yeah." I took a long swig of beer and stretched like a cat in the dying sun. "So how are the photos coming along?"

"Well enough. I have a feeling I could get these published." She handed me the cigar and I handed her the beer. "And your painting? Is W helping you out?"

I shrugged and puffed on the cigar. "Seems like it." I pointed at the horizon. "It's about time for him to make an appearance."

"Good, I'd like to meet the new boyfriend. See if he gets the Red stamp of approval."

I laughed. "I'm totally fucking nuts."

"Hey, is your mom nuts?"

"No. I told you, she's by-the-book middle-class normal."

"Do you want to be like your mom?"

"Hell no."

"Then good thing you're nuts. Your mom doesn't paint. She doesn't have weird-ass friends. She's stays sad and boring, from what you've told me, and you're happy enough not being boring."

I raised the cigar. "Here's to being happy enough."

After we'd finished the cigar and the beer and were climbing back through the window, I realized that it was twilight. I started looking around.

"W!" I whispered.

"You don't have to whisper," said Red. "There are no secrets here." She turned and yelled up at the ceiling. "Hey W! My name's Red! I look scary but I'm kind of nice! Want to come out?"

I turned around and suddenly the whole fake wall that Red had built was covered in W and the shadows that came from him. His head was tilted down, and though he didn't really have eyes, I felt like they were closed. Looking closer, his chest and arms were covered in strips of dark gold.

"Did you see that?" Red asked. "The lights just flickered. Creepy."

I walked up to him. "W? Are you alright?"

He looked up at me and his body stretched against the wall. "Em," he said, his voice vibrating through my chest. "I feel so weak."

"What's happened to you?"

"The most amazing things," he whispered. "You've done the most amazing things to me. And I trust you. What's left of me, this little shred of me that still holds any semblance of who or what I am, it trusts you so completely. You have set my heart aflame, and I am becoming more flame than heart, yet they were always the same thing, in the beginning, heart and flame."

I reached up and touched his face. "Do you have enough energy to meet someone?"

He looked over my shoulder. "She cannot see me, Em."

"But she believes in you. She knows that you are here."

"Of course, Em. I would do anything you ask." He raised his voice. "Hello, Red. My name is W. I am pleased to meet you."

I turned my head. "He said hello and introduced himself."

"Um, hello Mr. W." She stepped up to where I was looking at him and stuck out her hand to shake. "My name's Red, but you can call me Red."

He reached out, leaned forward and placed his hand around hers and the lights flickered again.

"That's kinda tripping me out," Red whispered to me.

"I think some days he has more energy than others," I said.

"Mr. W," said Red. "Do you have enough energy to do something to me? Maybe a tap on the shoulder or give me a push or something?"

W looked at me and shook his head. "I... I'm not sure how safe that would be."

"He says he doesn't know if it's safe."

Red shook her head. "Do it. Please."

I caught W's eyes and nodded to him.

chapter 18

All I could see was light – oranges and yellows and whites bent and curved into the shape of walls and a couch and a table, lights bent and curved into shapes that made up Em and Red. The only darkness I saw was a tree made of shadow that stretched up through the center of Em, and small black stars that hovered about the photographs that were hanging from clotheslines in the room behind me.

Em looked up at me and nodded. It hurt to look directly into her eyes, the light coming from them was so bright and hot that it made my face ache.

"I need you to turn the music back on," I said.

I lowered myself to the ground, my whole chest sore like a healing wound, and Em turned the stereo on. The beats began emerging from the speakers, the white cotton-ball flurries of noise large and quick.

"Turn the volume down," I said, and she did so. The flurries reduced in size and slowed down as they rolled in chaotic circles across the floor. "Down a little more." I lowered down and held out my open hand and a flurry the size of a golf ball came up to me, sniffing my hand suspiciously. With my other hand I patted the top of it and it rolled up into my hand, nuzzling my palm and thumb. I floated around Red, my cape of light dripping off the wall to follow me.

"Stay close to her," I said to Em, "and be ready. But don't stand too close."

"Be ready for what?" asked Em.

"I don't know."

"Maybe we shouldn't do this," said Em.

Red turned to Em and put a hand on her shoulder. "All we have are our passions and our opportunities. If this is real, then people don't get this opportunity, and I don't want to give it up and wonder what would have happened."

Em stepped back. "Do it, W."

I pet the flurry and held it close to my lips, crouching down so that it would hit Red's torso rather than her face, in case the effect was physical. I blew on the flurry and it began shaking, letting out a high-pitched hum, and then it shot out at Red. Her shirt of light quivered against her skin and her head reeled backwards as the flurry vanished into her. A loud whisper escaped her lips, something that sounded like a long, drawn out "Oh."

Em yelled out her name as Red fell backwards, smoky yellow light spilling from her stomach, and Em caught her and lowered her to the floor.

"Red? Red?"

Em had Red's head in her lap. The little flurries seemed more agitated as they rolled around the floor. But were they agitated because of what I'd done or were they picking up on Em's mood?

"She's not waking up!" Em yelled. "I think she's breathing. Shit!"

I swam forward next to Em, took her hands and placed them over the hole where the yellow smoke was spilling out.

"W!" she yelled. "Do something!"

I reached my hand into Em's chest, touching the shadowy tree growing inside of her, which was so cold that it hurt the tips of my fingers. The shadow leaked through my skin and up into my arm and shoulder as Em began coughing and trying to pull away. With my other hand I held her hands against Red's stomach, and when the shadow had seeped up my neck, over my jaw and across my lips I bent down and touched my mouth to Em's hands and breathed into them.

Red's torso raised into the air as her back arched, and I felt so many feathers springing up against my lips. Then I pulled away and gasped for air, though as far as I knew I'd never needed to breathe air before. Letting go of Em's hands, we both fell backwards heaving onto the floor, and Red began coughing.

The yellows and oranges of light were shifting back and forth on the ceiling to the soft throbbing of the music.

"Jesus!" I heard Red say. "Oh, man!"

I looked over and Em was lying on her back, looking up at the ceiling. "Rip me apart," she whispered.

"Em," I said.

She looked over at me with those searing white eyes. "I know what comes next." Then she sat up quickly, shaking her head. "Red, are you alright? Red?"

I floated back into the air, looking down at them. Red was sitting up, looking down at her stomach. "Em, there are small, black feathers all over my shirt. I feel like I just went bungee jumping." She put a hand on her own chest. "Whoa. My whole body's woozy."

"Red," Em whispered, "meet W."

Red looked at Em, and Em's smile faded away.

"I think I'm gonna go get a drink," said Red.

"Are you alright?"

Red nodded slowly. "I'm good." She looked down at the feathers, which to me were made of yellow light. "Can I keep some of these?"

"Keep all you want, I have enough at my place."

"Em, thank you. For letting me try that."

"I'm just glad you're OK."

"Me too. You want a drink?"

"Um. I'll go if you want me to, but I just figured out the next step for the piece I'm working on, and I'm kinda itching to get back to it."

"You go on," said Red. "I don't feel like I'll be much of a conversationalist for at least an hour or two anyway. Gotta process some shit. That was intense."

Em got up and helped Red to her feet. "I'll have one drink with you."

"Passions and opportunities... You go and work. If I pass out, I'll call you."

"Ah – don't say that."

"Em, remember – I used to function on all kinds of drugs. I think I'll be OK with the residual effects of encountering your alter-ego-painting-guy. Be sure to thank him for me."

Em looked around, her eyes passing right over me. "He's either gone or invisible, but I have a feeling he heard you." She picked up her bag, then grabbed Red and hugged her. "Be safe. And call if you start feeling weird."

# chapter 19

I was about to walk out the door, but turned back to Red. "You're not planning on riding your skateboard tonight, are you?"

"Haven't used it for months. Take it."

The humming of the wheels on the street vibrated up through my sneakers and into the bones of my feet as I rode through the chilly night air, circling the potholes. I took another route to bypass The Duke's house because I didn't want to tell him I was skating home after dark. I found myself almost missing having drab, normal days. *Maybe I* should *go to work tomorrow*, I thought to myself. *It might help me normal out.*

It was about an hour's skate to get back to my own neighborhood. After I passed through Red and Duke's neighborhood, I was in the business district. I'd always liked going through the business district at night – all the tall, empty skeletal buildings, hollow of life and meaning. All of the business parks were full of abstract sculptures and trimmed bushes and trees, archaic looking fountains and tall obelisks – designed to give the workers a space outside of their cubicles or offices which had some kind of nourishment for the other half of their brains, all in a desperate hope that these structures and plants would lessen the number of nervous breakdowns and unhappy employees.

Halfway through the business district I swore that I heard music. I stopped and listened, and there was definitely the booming of a drum with some kind of horn, maybe a clarinet. I picked up the skateboard and walked between two huge office buildings, towards the music. I passed through a surreal business park which had a creek carved into the stone ground, a pyramid to one side of me and a hill of grass and trees on the other. The music grew louder as I walked through the empty park and around another building, and I realized that I was hearing the distinct, playful bobbing of circus music. I stopped and looked up. The music was definitely coming from one of the building tops above me, one of which was a parking garage.

I went into the parking garage, and when the elevator didn't seem to work I went into the stairwell and took the stairs to the roof. I opened the exit door a crack and peaked outside, but didn't see anything, though the music *was* much louder. From this close, I could tell that the music was layered with all kinds of horns, and I even heard a violin, xylophone and accordion. I peaked out further, then stepped out and closed the door quietly behind me. The music came from in front of me, but all I saw was the concrete rail bordering the parking garage roof and the buildings beyond with the star-filled night sky above them.

Edging up to the stone railing, I was left frozen and thoughtless by what I saw on the roof of the next building. There was a bald man with a long red-and-white-checkered trench coat, his back to me, waving his arms like a frantic conductor to instruments that seemed to be played by blurs of white light. The song itself, as much as the visual, stirred in me something very wild and primal and wondrous. All at once I needed to know who he was. The music reached up to me and gripped my beating heart in its hands, and I had to hold onto the rail to keep from falling over. And then, very suddenly, the song roared up to climax into three heavy bursts and ended. The man was heaving, and my ears were ringing in the sudden quiet of night.

He peered over his shoulder at me. His bald head was painted white, his face painted in yellows and reds and blues. I froze, wondering if I should say something or not, but he turned back and began conducting the next song, which sounded light and jovial, yet had a darkness running around underneath its covers.

I sensed something behind me and turned. Someone was climbing down off of the little building that housed the elevator and the door to the stairs. My hand reached into my shoulder bag and wrapped around my mace, and when the person got closer I saw that it was Matt.

He nodded to me, and mixed into his deep green eyes was a look of mistrust. "He never talks," said Matt. "Just conducts for hours, then leaves. Doesn't come back for a month, not until the next new moon."

"How'd you find him?"

"I come up here to play music sometimes. One night he was already playing over there when I got here."

"Is he like us?"

Matt shrugged. "I think so."

I looked back at the man. "Do you know what those white things are?"

"What do you mean?"

"The smudges holding the instruments."

"I... I only see instruments."

The man raised his arms to the sky and the playful music blossomed before him, then he turned around completely, and he had on the makeup of a clown – a huge, smiling red mouth around his real mouth, yellow triangles over his eyes and four blue tears painted on one cheek. He pulled on the lapels of his coat, the music continuing behind him, and leaped impossibly high into the air, his coat flapping madly behind him as he slowed down and landed right in front of us, balancing on the concrete rail. We both stepped back as the man squatted down on the railing. His bow tie was bright green, his pants striped and his shoes shiny black. Up close it was easy to see that he was very old beneath the makeup, though his blue eyes were intensely vibrant. He stuck out a white-gloved hand to me. "My name," he said in a deep, grave voice, "is Inconsequential. Pleased to meet your acquaintances."

If it had been any other night during any other week, I might not have been able to fathom this. But since it wasn't any other night or week, I shook his hand. "I'm Em."

He took my hand, brought it to his lips and kissed it. Then he turned his hand in the air, pulled a daisy out of nowhere and handed it to me. "A leaf for each heart you've broken, madame, and a petal for each one you've yet to break."

I accepted the flower and he looked next to me and raised an eyebrow. "You're looking a little worse for ware, my friend," he said, but Matt was to the other side of me. I looked, and Inconsequential was talking to empty space. He stuck out his hand and shook hands with nothing. "Newly severed, newly wed. If you wait until all of this makes sense, monsieur, you will see the end of time and have... *nothing! Nothing*, to show for it!" He smiled, then his face dropped into a wrinkled scowl.

Inconsequential stood up on the rail and looked up at the stars.

"So howl at the moon, that it may come out one more time." He turned towards the playing instruments. "They get sloppy if I'm away too long."

"Hey, how come you won't talk to me?" asked Matt.

The man in the checkered coat turned his white-painted, bald head, but not enough to actually look at Matt. "This is the only time I will speak to you, so listen well. You, boy, are useless... and a coward!"

The man leaped back over to the next roof, moving much too slow through the night air. His extension must have been helping him somehow. I turned towards the space where he shook hands with nothing. "W? How come he can see you but I can't?" I peered into the space, trying to see him. A strange pang ran through me, and as I looked back towards Inconsequential's dramatic conducting, I realized that what I felt was jealousy. It hurt me that this man in makeup, this complete stranger, had more access to W than I had. *I must speak to him,* I thought. *I want to see W all of the time.*

"Fuck that guy," said Matt. "Fuck you, Em, and fuck your extension. I wouldn't be surprised if right now Om is protecting me from him again." He turned to leave.

"What do you mean?"

"Oh, he didn't mention it? He tried to hurt me and Om stopped him, then he hurt her real bad. The same day you eighty-sixed me."

*Oh yeah,* I thought. *I did do that, didn't I?* "Well, I'm kind of a jackass... but you *were* freaking annoying. You're not eighty-sixed, Ok? I didn't tell anyone not to serve you. As for W and Om, I don't know what to say – I'm in the dark, remember? You know a hell of a lot more than I do, and you won't tell me anything. So maybe this clown guy will."

He stuffed his hands into the pockets of his corduroy jacket. "Hope it works out for you." He turned and walked away.

My hands wanted to clench into fists, but I still held the flower in one of them. "Well he's got one thing right! You *are* a coward!"

He walked through the door to the stairwell and was gone.

I turned around and gripped the concrete railing with my empty hand, letting the roughness of the stone tear at my fingertips. I knew he wasn't trying to be an asshole, but he was so freaking annoying. Why wouldn't he just talk to me? I shook my head, trying to get every shred of Matt out of my thoughts. "Screw him."

Slipping the daisy into a buttonhole of my shirt, I concentrated on Inconsequential, on his movements, looking for some hint, something he was doing that I was not. The man might never speak to me again, and I may never see him again, so that moment could have been all I had.

The music seemed to follow not only his exaggerated movements, but even the bending of his fingers, the sliding of his coat sleeves down his arms when his hands were raised, the waning of his body in what looked like exhaustion or even intoxication. It dawned on me the more I watched that every movement, however sloppy, was so entirely well planned that it skated along the edge of an absurd breed of obsession. I tried to picture where his extension would be – if it would be above him, feeding itself into him somehow, or perhaps in front of him, like he was channeling himself through it and out to those strange white blurs, those ghosts of blank energy. I wondered if he could see his own extension. Surely he must be able to. Maybe to him those white blurs were not blurs at all but people conjured up from the past, or from his imagination, or maybe they were somehow pieces of his extension.

Song after song he conducted, and not all were circus songs – some were polkas, some waltzes, some were what I thought might be klezmer, reminding me of a Bar Mitzvah I'd gone to long ago. Inconsequential even turned and started belting out opera with his raspy voice during one song, all for his one-person audience, and I couldn't tell if he was singing in English or not. I began clapping louder and louder after each song, and climbed up to sit on the concrete railing. After he sang opera I hollered and whistled at him - he smirked up at me before turning around to start up the next song.

And then it was over, and the white blurs were packing the instruments into their respective cases. Inconsequential walked to the edge of his roof, and my heart skipped as he leaped off the edge towards me, impossibly high so that he traveled over the rail and behind me. I turned around and he was falling very slowly, inch upon inch, yet his coat was flapping wildly as if he was falling quite quickly.

"How are you doing that?"

"Of all the questions, you ask the trivial." His feet finally touched the ground. "Your acquaintance, Monsieur W, he is floating in the air as we speak. Does he hide such things from you?"

"No, of course not, but..."

"Well who do you think he is, really? Are you him, is he you?!"
His arms shot up to the sky and his voice echoed back from the
office buildings. "Are we all not the same creature with *hundreds of*
*thousands of heads?!* Tear our eyes from the moon, that we may
drown in the sadness of dying worlds!" He began pacing back and
forth, gesturing madly as he yelled out. "The single dying point of
light left, from it is born such a vessel of music which only three
species of bird can remember, and even *they* cannot hope to ever
play such a thing!" He turned to me and raised an eyebrow. "Ah,
yes, the girl. I get worked up while rehearsing." He pulled a small
white card out of the air and handed it to me. "If you would wish to
come and meet with me, this is where I am sometimes. But *do not*
let that boy or his *other* look at this card. Nor any other friend or
acquaintance. I am incredibly picky about who or what I let know
my whereabouts."

I took the card from him. It said:

### ARKAN'S VAULT
*Books Collectibles Memories*
*And Other Things of No Value*

The address was on Main Street downtown, around all the
antique stores.

"I'd say you could come by as soon as tomorrow," he said, then
glanced beside me, "but due to the state of your acquaintance, I
assume the earliest I'd see you is next week."

"How come you think Matt's useless? I mean, annoying, sure.
And introverted. I just met him and I've said some mean things to
him. But useless?"

"Perhaps I don't think that at all," said the man as he hopped
up onto the stone railing. "Maybe it's just what he needs to hear."
He pulled on the lapels of his coat. "He might make a fine a
doorstop, for example, if you threw a blanket over him." He turned
and bowed to me. "Madame, I bid thee adieu." And then he was
soaring back across the gap between the buildings.

Rhythms and vocal charms spouting from the instruments, each of the players so willingly giving themselves to Inconsequential's spell, making his will their own. Everything was still coated with brilliant yellows and oranges. There were no flurries of vibration, as if the music being created was so raw, so close to the primal center of music's beginnings as to be free of reality's grip, sustaining itself in some sort of vacuum. Like what was being played was the *concept* of music, the emotions at the heart before it becomes vibration.

Below us Inconsequential waved his hands in the air, commanding the players. He seemed to me almost a creature rather than a man. Looking at him was like looking at four or five of him layered atop each other, all dressed slightly different, all with different expressions and body language, and each had a different level of consistency. The least solid of them was the easiest for me to see, for this version of him looked to be made of liquid and often moved before the rest of them, or began moving in a different direction altogether. I thought it could be his extension, since I didn't see anything else that could have been it, unless the players themselves were his extension divided up into separate entities.

As for the players, they were the strangest thing I had seen yet in my short existence. So strange, in fact, that I had a hard time even looking at them. To gaze upon the dozen of them was to gaze into a dozen holes in time, or gazing at slices of different times stacked up atop each other. I saw, heard and smelled smoky jazz clubs and raucous circus tents, speakeasies and joyous weddings and camp fires circled by dancing, singing families. The first time I gazed at them I fell to the ground with the world spinning around me.

It was then that Matt had walked up and began speaking to Em.

I had to search around behind him through all of the streaming light before I saw Om, floating near the far edge of the parking garage. I made sure to keep my distance from Matt and kept an eye on Om during the strange evening. I wondered if she was just keeping her distance because of me, or if she wanted to keep her eyes from falling onto the players.

Afterwords, while I held onto Em's bag as she skated away from the parking garage, between the large buildings and then into the other neighborhoods, I felt energy gathering inside of me. My fingers dug into the fabric of her bag as I floated behind her like trailing flag, like a ghost or phantom of something unfinished, something not completely realized. There was a beating within – the symbols which had rearranged my insides and then solidified were throbbing in my chest, and their beat was vibrating up to my shoulders and down my arms, wanting – needing – to enact myself on my creator. I struggled to hold these feelings at bay, trying not to affect her while she was out in the world, yet I found the distinction between her room and the rest of the world starting to fade. It was all drenched in orange and yellow light, it was all the same place, made of the same materials. But no, she needed the painting, didn't she? And her tools.

Finally she got to the door by the convenient store and unlocked it, but I was shaking. I questioned my judgment – maybe I should not have waited. I felt empty of life, like I'd bled to death and my insides were dry and shriveling up. My muscles ached as I crawled up her glowing form while she ascended the stairs, and I reached her shoulders as she stepped through her door. In a violent shiver the feathers fell from my body, floating down about the floor. My body was on fire.

Em reached down and picked up one of the feathers. "W?"

I pulled her head back until she was looking at the ceiling, then I looked down into her eyes, the piercing light coming from them searing my own, but I held their gaze because I knew that the burning was one of the last things I would ever feel. My tears were not made of light – they were the darkest blue as they spilled down onto her glowing cheeks, her forehead, her lips. And where they fell, small blossoms and leaves of gold sprouted, bursting from her skin of light as her face contorted with pain below me, but I held her head in that place, neither letting her nor myself avert our gazes. And when the blue liquid splashed into her eyes, her lips parted as the golden leaves sprouted from the edges of her eyelids.

"My life," I muttered, and her eyes met mine as she truly saw me, tears of light flowing down her face. I kissed the leaves on her forehead. "It's time for you to finish killing me, Em."

She reached up and pulled my forehead against hers. I swam around so that my body faced hers as she picked up a paint brush from the table. Her head leaned into my chest, the golden leaves scratching lightly at my skin – and they were slowly growing in twirling patterns away from her face, all from where my tears had touched her skin.

"Close your eyes," she whispered.

"No." It was the first and last thing I would deny her.

She stepped back and pressed the wooden end of the paint brush deep into my chest. When I looked into her face then, I knew that this was another part of her peering at me from beneath the golden foliage. This was not the Em that worked in a coffee shop or the Em that loved artwork or even the Em that liked to dance to music in her room. This was the Em that I didn't know. This was the Em that Em didn't know. She cried as the blue gore gushed from my chest, yet her eyes were fierce and certain, and there were no words that would pass between us. Silence filled the room along with my blood.

Gravity dragged me slowly down, my knees buckling underneath me as I fell onto them. But I kept her gaze the whole time. I did not need to tell her that I trusted her. Or that I loved her.

The light that had covered everything began to fade away and die, and soon only the slowly twirling, growing leaves and vines were there against the darkness.

The vines and leaves moved further away. I heard the gentle clink of ice in a glass, and then the sound of liquid being poured. Then even that was gone, and I was dead.

# chapter 21

For days and days I holed up in my apartment and created. Since Red had come back early from her trip, she was glad to take all of my shifts at the coffee shop. She would usually come by to see me before or after the shifts, and I would cover my work with a sheet. I was excited, but scared. I hadn't seen W since Red's apartment. There had been a small pile of gold-painted leaves on my floor after the night of the parking garage, next to a large puddle of dark blue paint. At twilight I could never find him. I checked the rooftop, even walked to The Cove once, but there was no sign of him. Yet so much creativity was flowing through me, and I was certain that W had something to do with it.

At first I was just eating frozen dinners I got from the convenience store, but when Red found this out she started bringing me take-out food from the area, usually Chinese or Italian. I never actually got hungry, but I was drinking pretty regularly and didn't want to get too drunk as I worked. And I didn't want to catch a cold or anything.

Not only did I not feel hunger, but I didn't feel lonely at all. When Red showed up I would have to make myself talk to her. I turned my cell phone's ringer off and didn't return any calls. If Red hadn't had a key to my apartment, my only social interactions would have been with Abid and the other employees of the convenience store. I found myself talking to W even though I couldn't see him – asking him questions about what materials I should use, or if the color needed to be brighter, or if it would look better if the lines curved another way.

After about five days I left the house to get some wood and nails from the hardware store, and to go to the park to collect leaves. The air was getting chilly with the approach of fall. The birds flew

back and forth between trees that were turning yellow and orange
with the cloudy sky at their backs. When you're hung over and
haven't been out in the sunlight for a few days, nothing looks real. I
felt like a scavenger in some wasteland that used to be a world, like
Bruce Willis in *Twelve Monkeys*. Seeing the kids playing in the park,
the people walking down the sidewalk, it was like looking at
memories of something I'd never actually seen, but only read about.
A time long since past.

And, like always, when I stepped into my apartment the piece
was calling to me from across the room. It existed in separate
sections - one part was on the easel, the other was propped up
against the wall. I took the leaves out of their garbage bag, careful
not to bend any of them, then cleared off some room on the floor
and started setting up the long two-by-twos that I would start nailing
together.

I boiled some water and ground up some coffee, then poured
both into the glass pitcher of my french press, the scent of the coffee
making me smile. I put on an Edith Piaf CD and sang along as much
as two semesters of high school French would allow, meanwhile
arranging the wood on the floor into the shape of a diamond which
would be nearly as tall as me. When the coffee was done brewing, I
fixed myself a cup.

Picking up one of the canvases, I placed it onto the diamond.
Both of the paintings, which would end up being one piece, were
larger than anything I'd painted before, but not by much, and one
was several inches larger than the other. The wood I'd gotten was
nearly the perfect size. I got out my hacksaw and began sawing and
nailing the diamond of wood together. When that was done, I stood
on a chair and hammered a large nail into the wall and hung the
diamond up. Then I took it down, nailed the slightly smaller
painting to the diamond and hung them both up on the wall.

A shiver ran through me. Something inside wanted to just sit
back and stare at what I'd done so far. I looked over my shoulder at
the painting of W lying on my bed. I had to keep moving – not to
rush myself, but to just keep a steady pace. It felt good. This act of
creation was filling me up. I felt as if the edges of me were being
stretched out. Like the outside parts of me were fading away, so that
only the center would remain.

I pulled my table up to the new piece and began opening up
jars of paint.

*          *          *

The clouds were puffy fields of lavender in the sky. The buildings were all cast in shades of dark blue. It was twilight, and there was no W on the rooftop of my apartment. But there was a Red.

"I think this chow mein beats the hell out of the other place," said Red. "It's from the Moon place. Moon Wok maybe."

"Sorry, everything still kinda tastes like styrofoam to me. I believe you though."

"Em." She was sitting up on the air conditioning unit, and I was standing next to it.

"What is it?"

"I... I support you completely. You know that, right?"

"Of course I do! When you see this piece, you'll understand." I'd never been so sure of my artwork before – yet I didn't think of it as egotistical, just that it was becoming exactly what I'd envisioned. Maybe even better.

"I just... well, I need you, Em. I mean, not now. I love that you're doing something important, something that you love. I just want to know that you'll come back. Back into my world."

I walked up to her, set both our take-out boxes down and took both her hands into mine. Her wild eyes looked into me and then calmed.

"Sorry," she said. "I just get paranoid about things sometimes."

"You're a part of my life, Red. I'll always be with you."

She let out a long sigh. "I know, girl. I'm silly, but it feels good to hear you say that."

I hugged her and her whole body relaxed against me. "Thanks," she said. "Since the other night when we were talking about your dad, I've been thinking a little too much about mine."

"Let's go somewhere soon. We'll get the same day off and go to one of the parks, or the lake."

I felt her nod against my neck. "That would be great."

I let her go and we started back on our dinners. The temperature was dropping along with the sunlight. I could hear the passing cars driving home after work, but I pretended it was the sound of the wind and that the whole world was gone, which wasn't as hard to do as it probably should have been.

*        *        *

I don't know if it was two, three or four days that passed. I was standing in my room, flecks golden paint dried and cracking on my arms and hands, staring at the two pieces. One was hanging on the wall with the diamond attached to it, the other was on the easel. It was almost complete.

I wrapped the wooden beams with thin black cloth, then took out an antique barber's shaving razor. It was covered in rust except for the sharpened blade, which gleamed like polished silver. I walked up to the piece on the easel, my heart pounding in my chest, and sliced across it.

chapter 22

Once the life had been bled from me, the only thing left was a darkness so dense, so complete and consuming that it drowned everything else. It was not empty space; it was not occupied space. It was not really space at all, but something primal, something so utterly unaffected by time, emotion or thought. The only thing inside of that thick, wondrous dark was me. I hadn't thought of myself as anything cumbersome or heavy until I saw myself against that ultimate backdrop of nothingness. And then the dark reached into me, sidestepping all of my imperfections, and grabbed onto the thing that was judging, the part of me that saw the contrast between myself and the dark. The moment it grabbed me, that judgmental part unraveled with a long, heavy sigh, and my whole being loosened. The dark went to each part of me, holding each piece like a sacred artifact and letting it unravel in its hands. Afterwards, the only thing left of me was something so thin and see-through that it almost refused to exist at all. I felt the dark moving through the places where the pieces of me had been, through the hollows and the caves, and something occurred to me: The dark and I were of the same material. Once I realized this, I was floating in myself, breathing myself in.

There was no longer any conception of time, of memory or of any kind of thought. Then, after what would later seem like years, the dark spoke to me. It's voice traveled through itself and through the center of me, reverberating outward and inward.

"Do you wish to go back?" it asked me, it asked itself, I asked myself.

I saw movies like floating television screens, depicting Em moving about her room, her life. "I could," I said. "Does it matter if I do *not* go back?"

"No," said the dark. "It does not matter. But if you do, you will have to pick up some of the pieces of you again, and your decision will *seem* to matter very much."

"It will matter to Em."

"You and her are the same. But if you go back, you will appear separate again."

"You spoke to me once before. In a parking lot, after I fought against Om."

"What is your decision?"

I watched the screens of Em floating before me. They flickered and slowly faded to white. "I wasn't finished. I'd like to go back."

The screens sputtered out and all was the dark again. I tried speaking to the dark, but there was no answer. So I waited, though I became quite fascinated with feeling the dark move in and through me, and it was nothing like waiting at all.

And then a thin sliver of yellow light was cut across the darkness. I moved towards it, cautious but curious. A second line appeared, creating an X. Then a third and a fourth, making an asterisk. I floated up to it, up to this hole in the fabric of the nothingness that had bled into me, that had become me. I reached out, and when my hand touched the star of light, the pieces of dark were peeled away before me, creating a deafening square of bright yellow light which wrapped itself around my hand and arm, pulling my arm through the opening. I fought to get away, but the relentless, malicious light dug into me and forced me further in, and once my head was in, I felt the light wrap like skin around my arms and my face, and I couldn't breathe. It pulled the rest of me through and I fell, clawing at my face to get the sheet of light off me. My shoulder cracked against some kind of ground.

I tried to scream out into the blinding light. My whole body throbbed and ached and was starved for too many things at once. Finally my fingers punctured the light-skin over my mouth and I breathed in the air, wheezing. I got a grip on it and tore it away from my nose and jaw, then tore it from my eyes and off of my head. At first all I could see was the skin all over my body, it was so blinding. I cried out, reaching out and latching onto the first thing I could find, holding onto it like an anchor. It was a small shoe, with a small foot inside of it.

Looking up, I saw Em there above me like a giant. She gazed forward, and following her eyes I saw her other hands holding up a canvas against another canvas, both face to face, and the one she held was all cut up. She pushed it forward and the canvas behind it pushed out the torn pieces of the first canvas until it revealed itself like an opening flower. She pulled each long triangle of torn canvas out and fastened it to a diamond of black cloth that was mounted behind both of the canvases.

Looking down at myself, I saw that there were tiny rips all over this skin of light, as if I was too large for it and it had begun to split open. Inside the rips was a deep, deep darkness. Then the skin began loosening and growing layers of itself, becoming like a large robe. I was no longer bound to the ground then, and floated up into the room. Long triangles of light and dark unraveled into the air from my shoulders and back.

Em picked up a thin brush covered in black paint and began adding to the two pieces that were now one. The black rips all across me shifted and curled, and I felt myself solidify inside the room as they became like strange writing or symbols all across me. When I looked at the painting, I knew that it was a painting of me – a painting of who I was now, not of who I had been. And that's when I knew I had a face and even hair, all the color of white ash. I reached up and felt my eyes, my eyelids and lashes.

"How strange," I whispered. "I have eyes now."

Then something inside convulsed and I doubled over in the air, falling and slamming into the ground, where I began to wretch.

# chapter 23

I was nearly finished with the new piece when I heard the most revolting sound and spun around. For a split second I thought a giant cat had gotten in through my window and was coughing up a humongous hairball. Then I thought something large and wet had fallen in through the roof and bright light was spilling in through the hole, but it was dark outside. I stepped back against the wall, knocking into the piece as I sheilded my eyes with one hand. The light had arms and legs and looked kind of like my painting, and it was puking up lots of green stuff.

"Holy shit!" I yelled, holding my stomach and averting my eyes. "Maybe next time you can tell me when you're gonna do that!" Even though I couldn't see it, I knew it had to be W.

It coughed and wiped its mouth and looked up at me as the light faded to a dim, shimmering gold. It's head, neck and face were white-gray and pasty. It kind of looked like W, and it kind of really didn't. There were golden leaves pressed into all of the gold parts of his body, and the black parts looked like liquid. But his face was the same shape.

"You have eyes," I said. "And hair. I don't know how I feel about that."

He looked right at me and a chill ran through my body. It was freaking creepy.

"I have eyes," he said, wiping the last of the green liquid off of his mouth. His voice was almost the same, yet somehow more regal, as if it held more authority. He pulled himself over to the wall and sat back against it, breathing deeply.

"It's good to see you." Half of me really wanted to give him a hug and while the other half didn't want to touch him. He was just so different.

He winced and nodded to the painting behind me. "Please. It's almost done."

Nodding, I went to the painting and kept working. At first I couldn't help but smirk, knowing that he was there behind me again, but soon the smirk faded as my hand marked the canvases and my mind traveled into the work. Before long the hand holding the brush fell to my side and I was done. I grabbed a knife from my table, cut off some strands of my hair, dipped them into the red paint and signed it in the corner: M.

When I turned around he was standing up, leaning against the wall, the long triangles of gold and black crawling out along the wall behind him like feelers or antennae. I picked up my Black Russian. I felt so good, and I barely even had a buzz. "So what do you think, W?"

"It's wonderful. Thank you."

I tongued the inside of my cheek. "You look like shit."

"Em..."

"I mean, you look good. Amazing, even. But you look like you *feel* like shit."

"I'm not..." He stepped towards me, his eyes creeping me out a little. "Em, I'm not the one you called W."

I raised an eyebrow. "What?"

He took another step towards me and I stepped back.

"You killed him," he said. "Remember?"

My palms were sweating and my hand clenched tight around my glass. "Then who the fuck are you? And why do you seem like W?"

"I'm..." He looked down at his hands as he turned them over. "I'm what's left of him. The remnants. The rest is how you've made me, shaped me, added to me."

I backed up into the door jam of my bathroom and sunk down to the ground. I set my glass on the floor and couldn't stop shaking. "I didn't kill him," I whispered. "You're just confused." But when I looked across the room at him, I knew that he was right. He was no longer W. I grabbed fistfuls of my hair. "I... I didn't know this was going to happen."

"You did," said the creature. "Something inside you knew."

I pulled myself up using the door jam. All of my muscles suddenly felt the soreness of days upon days of drinking along with the atrophy of not moving around enough. My forehead pressed against the door jam. "What do I call you?"

I closed my eyes, and for a moment I thought maybe he'd disappeared. But then he spoke: "You gave me the same name – you've named me W."

Walking into the bathroom, I slammed the door shut and locked it. I pulled open the shower curtain, ran the water, threw off my clothes and stepped inside. When my eyes shut, the water became my skin – a moving and living cover keeping my insides from falling out of me. I leaned against the tiled shower wall, feeling the cold tiles press against me.

I couldn't have killed him, but inside I knew that I had. But why would I need to destroy him just to create something new? And why couldn't I remember? Did he know I was going to do that to him, or did he feel like I turned against him?

Tears mixed with the hot water running over my face. "I'm so sorry," I whispered. "I didn't want this. I didn't mean for this to happen." I sat down and buried my head in my knees, hugging my legs.

Imagining his voice, I tried to conjure him up, but all that came to me in the dark behind my eyes were blurred images of him and incoherent whisperings. None of it made any sense – no matter how many questions I asked in my head, none of them were answered. I didn't want to believe that I did anything to W, but I could almost remember hurting him, and I could almost remember him asking me or even telling me to do it. But how could I trust myself or any kind of memory that I had? I'd just killed someone close to me and couldn't remember any of it, and all I had left was a few pieces of him and this horrible feeling inside.

It hadn't been two weeks since I'd met W, and I'd changed and learned so much in that time. I thought he'd be with me until I died. He'd always said that he didn't think he'd ever be able to leave.

My thoughts bled out through my eyes and mouth, swirling into the warm water and down the drain until I was only a body there, curled up lying on the shower floor, letting the now-cold water beat lightly onto my skin.

Eventually I got up and turned off the shower. My whole body was numb from the cold, but the air was still thick with steam. I wiped the moisture from the mirror and looked into my pink eyes. "Who are you?" I whispered.

My face grew pale, my hair grew quickly down to my

shoulders and then turned into shadow and my lips darkened to purple. My eyes and eyebrows vanished and all the space around them deepened with shadow until they too were a deep, dark purple. My breath caught in my throat and I fell backwards onto the floor and screamed.

The bathroom door burst open, the hook-lock snapping off the door frame. "Em, are you alright?"

I looked up at the abomination, the thing that I'd made out of pieces I'd cut out of my friend. I yanked the towel off the towel rack and covered myself as I stood up. "Leave me."

"Em, I don't think you understand quite..."

I stepped up to him, looked right into those ash-gray eyes. *"Get... the fuck... away from me."*

He left and I slammed the door shut.

chapter 24

The starlight made hundreds of tiny pinpricks across my skin, and the lights coming up from the streets bathed the walls of the surrounding buildings in neons and florescents. I found it strange how much more space I took up than before, the torn streams of gold and shadow constantly stretching out, feeling out every surface, drinking up the moisture in the air left over from the week's rain. Em was down there sleeping. I didn't know if I would ever vanish from her again. I came out of the painting after twilight, and she still saw me when I went to see why she screamed in the bathroom.

I didn't understand why she was upset. Maybe she didn't understand what I said, but she should know, shouldn't she? Weren't we the same creature? Isn't this just part of her own plan?

I would do as she asked, and keep my distance from her for a while. But staying on the outskirts of her world wouldn't last for long. That's not what I came back to do, and it saddened me that she had such anger towards me.

Clouds stretched and ballooned into each other as they moved across the sky, never completely blocking out the starlight, which was finally snuffed out by the coming of dawn. I jumped down onto the rooftop, paced back and forth along the edge. So much energy burned through me, but what little there was of my old self urged me to keep the energy inside, to pacify it, keep it at bay until Em was ready for it.

"This won't last," I said to the old parts of me. "You barely hold any meaning anymore. This energy wants to move into Em, through me. If she hadn't asked me to stay away from her, I wouldn't be listening to you at all. I know my purpose. I know why she created me."

I lifted into the air, letting the rising sun reach into the golden layers of leaves that served as my flesh, toying with the energy inside of me, plucking me like the strings of a cello. I felt Em asleep so far below me, her dreams cloudy and covered in shadow. There was so much less of me inside, and I almost didn't know how to navigate in the utter simplicity. The empty space inside and out was so vast as to be beyond comprehension.

So I floated there, above her building, soaked in sunlight and feeling the vastness all throughout and around me. The sun was high above me when she finally left the apartment. I followed her, and when she sat down on the bus stop bench she looked around, and I knew she was looking for me, but her eyes passed me right over.

# chapter 25

Downtown was the oldest part of the city. The buildings were all brick and pillars and stone, each carrying histories that, if they were interesting enough, were spouted out by the guides of the walking tours. I'd never been on a walking tour, but I'd heard bits and pieces the handful of times I'd walked past the tours.

The air was a little warmer than it had been the last few days, and it didn't look like it would be raining for a while. I was glad that the creature had left me alone for the time being. I didn't sleep well at all, woke up with an aching head and muscles. When I saw the new piece, something shifted inside of me. It reached towards me, pulling at the butterflies in my stomach, drawing them out into the air between us. There was no denying that it was better than the other piece. How could something that felt so right come out of something that felt so fucked up? I had to get out of the apartment and turn my head off for a while. I'd grabbed my headphones and a Goldfrapp CD and left for the bus stop.

Walking across downtown now, I listened to the layers of operatic vocals spread over synthesized beats. I hadn't even thought about where I was going to get off the bus, but as soon as I stepped onto the downtown sidewalk I remembered Inconsequential's card, which I'd left in my other bag. I knew the place was on Main Street though, and figured I'd find it eventually.

As I made my way down the cobblestone sidewalks, I passed the light posts, the old-fashioned signs for antique stores hanging by big black chains, the buildings made up of the oldest bricks in the city. With the music pulsing through my headphones, I walked through my own world, hardly an active participant in anything happening around me.

Something darted in front of me on the ground and I almost

tripped while trying to avoid kicking it. I grabbed onto a brick wall to keep from falling, then saw the small gray cat that had run out of an alley.

"Ought to be careful," I said to it.

It was hiding under a parked car, sticking its head out and looking at me. I crouched down and held out my hand, but it just stared with its bright yellow eyes. I turned and looked into the small alley it had run out of and there was a sign hanging above a door: Arkan's Vault.

I turned back to the cat. "Thanks."

*          *          *

The air inside the shop was thick with smells of age and paper. Dust danced in the light of the lamps which lit the messy shelves and piles of books. Static-ridden piano music drifted throughout the shop, and when I finally made my way through the labyrinth of shelves and up to the empty desk, I found that the source of the music was an old vintage radio, maybe from the fifties.

"Sorry, miss, I didn't see you arrive," said a man behind me.

I turned and an old man was approaching. He stood at least a foot taller than me, and his skin was tanned and creased. He wore a brown brimmed hat and a brown suit. When he saw my face he stopped. "Ah. Enter the girl."

"If I'd seen you on the street I wouldn't have recognized you."

He turned and disappeared behind some bookshelves. "That's because I'm in costume at the moment."

I heard door locks sliding into place, which was a little creepy. I reached into my pocket to assure myself that my mace was there, just in case.

"What about your other customers?" I asked.

"No one can find us in this blasted alley," he said, reappearing. "Besides, the word 'Vault' is in the title of the shop, which carries with it a few implications, least of which is that the door will be locked from time to time." He walked around me and turned the volume down on the radio. "I've long ago lost the patience for Chopin."

I found my eyes glancing over some mail that was scattered on the desk. He quickly gathered it up and turned it around before I could see the name on the envelopes.

"Ah-ah," he said. "You don't want to know my pretend name, just as I don't want to know yours."

"I only have one name."

"No you don't. No one names their child after a letter of the alphabet." His eyes ran along the back of his hand. "Well, I suppose I did, once. But it was not an alphabet anyone had heard for a long, long time."

I hadn't really thought about it before, but I hadn't gone by my given name since I was little. "I guess you're right."

"Would you like some tea while we chat?"

He led me up a thin set of stairs that spiraled up into a circular hole in the wooden ceiling. Upstairs was a small room with windows that looked out over Main Street. There were old, empty cages hanging from the ceiling, and the shelves lining the walls were full of knickknacks and vases and ornate boxes.

"Please, have a seat," said Inconsequential as he disappeared into the next room. There was a well-organized desk against one wall, a couch and two cushioned chairs around a short table against another. I sat on the couch and looked about the room, waiting for him to come back. There was a painting of a worn and broken street with a group of people in torn clothes walking past old buildings, obviously vacating, carrying bags and sacks. They all looked worn and jaded, and I crossed the room for a closer look. It was subtle, since their faces were all in shadow, but they were each wearing a different kind of clown makeup.

"I hope you like liquorice tea," said Inconsequential from behind me. "If not for its taste, than surely for its medicinal qualities."

He'd removed his hat and, with his bald head, looked a little more like he had when I'd seen him the other night. I still wouldn't have recognized him on the street.

"I like liquorice," I said.

He brought two tea cups and a tea pot over to the desk. He glanced over at the sofa. "I can't sit on those damned things any longer. Last time I did, I wasn't able to walk for a week. Pull up one of those chairs."

I did so and sat facing him as he poured the tea and sat himself across the desk from me. "Who painted that?" I asked as I sipped my tea.

He barely glanced at it. "A woman painted it for me. Many

lifetimes ago."

"It's beautiful."

"It is." He inhaled the steam billowing up from his cup. "Now, madame, what has become of your friend?"

"You mean W?" I asked, and my heart sank when I uttered his name.

"Yes, the W character. Have you finished what you were working on?"

I set the tea down on the desk and buried my face in my hands. "Give me a minute," I whispered.

There was a loud *slam* and I jumped back in my chair.

"Jesus!" I yelled out. There was a large brown book lying on the floor. "What did you do that for?"

His blue eyes were spears pointed at me. "I'm giving you a minute. So go ahead, wallow in your misery. Don't let me distract you with my strange habit of tossing heavy books onto the ground."

I just stared at him.

"Em, please," he said. "Please go on. I'm sure your life is very hard." He folded his hands on the desk. "But could you pick that book up for me? I would, but my back isn't what it used to be."

I stared at him for a moment, then picked up the book, which was incredibly heavy. "Ever been told you're an asshole?" I asked, tonguing the inside of my cheek.

"Only by people I've met. Which is a surprisingly low number if you take into consideration both my age and the number of people on the planet."

Looking down at the book, the title was in raised gold and read, *The Heart*. "What is this?"

"That is the only book that I allow into this room. The title and contents change depending on the person holding it and what they need to learn most."

"Oh yeah?" I opened it up to a random page. "Um, it's all in Russian."

"I guess you'd better start learning Russian then."

I looked up at the scowl etched into his stone face and I instantly burst out laughing.

He smiled. "Her eyes are alive again."

I set the book down and sipped my tea. "Um," I started, but stopped and thought for a moment. "I... I killed W, kind of. I didn't see him for about a week, and in that week I created a new piece, something better than anything I've ever made. Then W came back, but he's completely different. He feels different, looks different. He's not the one that I'd come to trust. He's someone else now – a stranger."

"How can that be? He's no stranger. Looking upon him should be like looking into a mirror."

"But it's not. It's like going to a new shrink that's read years worth of your files. He knows more about me than I do, I can sense it. And I don't think I can trust him."

"Are you afraid of letting yourself love him? Or do you know deep down that once you love him completely you will have to kill him, and that he'll come back as something else, another aspect?"

"Fuck, is that true? I can't do this again."

The man shrugged. "As long as you run from that fear, the fear will act as your truth, and the real truth will not matter. You ask what is really true? Only you can answer that for yourself."

I felt the heat of the mug against my palms. "Have you had to kill your extension?"

"The moon shines on us all, but how the individual meets the moon's light is completely unique to them. The real truth, the reality of it all, lies not in us nor in the moon itself, but rather in the conversation that occurs in the space between."

"What does that mean?"

"It means that my experience is so different than yours, that the question you ask is irrelevant to me. Perhaps I have, but did not see it as killing. Perhaps I have not, and for me that is something I've yet to experience."

He glanced next to me. "Your friend is here now. He is quite the stunning creature."

"You can see your... friend... all the time?"

He didn't answer me.

"I really want to see W all the time," I said.

"Yeah? And how's that working out for you?"

"What?"

"Wanting what you don't have. You're already a few steps ahead of most of the population, being able to have full conversations with aspects of yourself that are otherwise hidden from you. Have you always been so greedy?"

I bit my lip. "I just want to figure all of this out."

Inconsequential sipped his tea. "Well, you have a glaringly

obvious doorway, even if you can't see it all of the time. If that is really what you truly want, you're running pretty low on excuses."

I nodded and leaned forward in my chair, running my hands through my hair. "I suppose you're right."

"Of course I am. I'm old, and old people are always right."

chapter 26

I held onto the top of the bus as it made its methodical pace through the streets of the city, then I let go and lifted into the air as Em exited the bus downtown. I felt the memories of the old W creep up in my head, along with the memories of Em. It occurred to me that I could access more clearly Em's memories than the old W could. I could bring up vivid pictures of her mother and father, all her friends back in her home town, many of the houses she'd lived in. I could feel the sadness she used to feel in her home town, letting it pulse through me. She'd been called scarecrow because she hardly ate anything and she started wearing her mismatched, stitched-up clothing, and because she shaved her head for the first time and her hair grew back sticking up every which way.

Everyone in school knew what her father had done, and they told her so with their eyes. So she stopped making eye contact with anyone except for a couple of friends, becoming a recluse, burying herself in books and sketchbooks and shunning most of her schoolwork.

Em knew that her mother had thought she was on drugs, though Em didn't end up experimenting with drugs until later in art school. Rather than saying anything to Em about her suspicions, her mother further perfected the art of pretending everything was fine. Em went to therapy, but her mother never did, and after six months Em gave up trying to have a real conversation with her.

I rose up into the air, stretching out between the old buildings, following above Em as she walked down the sidewalk. Tiny pinpricks of noise crawled continuously out of her headphones like ants, moving down around her jaw and neck and then vanishing after a few moments. A ball of smoke darted out in front of her and underneath a car, and Em was startled and nearly fell. The smoke quickly morphed into the shape of a cat and peaked out at her. Floating down, I watched them make eye contact. Smoke billowed from the cat, especially when it moved. I was sure that the cat would disperse into the air if Em touched it.

She looked back into the alley the cat had come from. Then she told the cat, "Thank you," and walked into the alley.

The smoke cat looked at me with pulsing yellow eyes.

"Who are you?" I asked.

It darted away, running across the street. Em went through a door in the alley, and I swam through the air after the cat, across the street, under cars and then up a tree and into an open window. It stopped in the middle of a sparsely furnished bedroom and looked back at me, it's eyes widening as I swam into the window after it. The cat darted straight for a wall and then ran vertically up the wall and through the ceiling. I followed it up several stories, tracing it by the wisps of smoke it left behind. When I got to the roof, it was running towards the edge. I quickly swam around it and stretched out my form, the gold and black strips of cloth blocking its path.

It stopped and glared at me defiantly.

"Who are you?" I asked.

*Meow.* It's tone was that of a question, as if it didn't know why I would be asking what I was asking, or why I'd be chasing it. It shook it's head and dissipated into a small cloud which was quickly stolen away by the wind. I followed the smoke with my eyes as it traveled over the other rooftops, but it broke up into so many pieces, each piece spread so thin, and I knew somehow that the cat was no longer in that smoke.

Like a lantern in the dark, I felt Em's presence tugging at me. I swam across the street and into the second floor of the building she'd entered, finding her sitting across a desk from Inconsequential, who once again was made up of many shifting layers, each with its own distinct solidity.

*           *           *

"Your friend is here now," said the most solid layer of the man. "He is quite a stunning creature."

What happened next is difficult to convey, and if I truly had a mind I'm sure the situation would have been even harder to deal with. The layers of Inconsequential became less attached to each other, and as the most solid of them stayed seated and continued speaking to Em, the others stood up. A cluster of them walked up to me, while one of them walked through a doorway, saying, "I'll make some tea," its voice sounding like a dying, whispered melody.

"Hello, Monsieur W," said the cluster of others. They stuck out their hands and I shook their hands all at once. The Inconsequential at the desk had no makeup on, yet his skin seemed to be slightly radiant. Some of the others didn't have makeup on, and some did, yet the makeup was crawling and shifting over their skin.

"How... how many of you are there?" I asked.

One of them smiled, and another one frowned. "There's only one of me," said the smiling one.

"Did... do you know of a cat, one that's made up of smoke?"

The smiling one raised an eyebrow. "Not off the top of my head. But there are a terrible amount of things that I do not know."

"A cat made of smoke came from your alley, that's how Em found her way here. Then I followed the cat for a while until it stopped being a cat and the smoke was blown away."

"Sounds like the world playing at your strings," said one of them, white and blue makeup rippling over its face. Even its eyes and nose were swimming along with the makeup, like looking at a reflection in a pool. "She can be a bitch, the world can, when she's in one of her moods. Now the moon! That's an astral body I'd live on if I didn't think I'd become more of a recluse than I already am. I've been in love with *her* for more years than I have memories."

I dropped to the ground, onto my feet, and had to hold one of the large chairs to keep my balance as vertigo began to take hold of me.

"Go ahead and sit down," said one of them. "The tea's almost ready."

I sat down in the cushioned chair, and my weight pressing into it was such a strange and new feeling. I felt so heavy suddenly, so bogged down by concepts and ideas. Perhaps I did have something of a mind. Perhaps I was going a little mad.

One of them sat across from me on the couch. It was the least substantial of all of them, and it was the one who'd gone to make the tea. Its shape was vaguely that of the human form, and its whole body was swimming with facial features and clown clothing and makeup. I had to look away. "I'm sorry," I said.

"Quite understandable," it hummed in its melodious voice. I

had a very vivid memory of Em as a little girl sitting on the floor and turning the crank on a jack-in-the-box. The simple little tune that came from the box before the clown popped out – that was the melody of this being's voice, like something was turning the crank on him somewhere when he spoke. Or like there was a constant melody playing in his head and when he spoke, his words merely followed the tune.

He handed me a large mug of tea, and the warmth against the skin of my hand made me shiver. "I... I've never felt that before. But... I remember it."

I closed my eyes. I saw and felt the hot mug in my hands in countless memories, but my hands were small and frail in the memories, and I was inside of Em's body. I shivered again and opened my eyes.

"Careful with that," hummed the swimming form across from me. "I made that tea especially for you. Sip it slow – sip it and know yourself now."

I sipped the tea, and the steaming liquid burned the cracked ash-skin of my lips, seared my tongue and traced a burning line down my throat and into my stomach. A flock of memories fluttered through me of Em drinking tea, but in each of the memories I was absent – I was Em. Suddenly it was like Em's consciousness was trying to squeeze inside of my head, but there wasn't room for it – my head was too simple for all those complicated pieces of her.

"Don't try to force things one way or the other," said the Inconsequential who was sitting across from me. "The only thing really happening is the drinking of tea."

The creature across from me, a swimming human-shaped canvas of body parts and paint, began to solidify a little as I sipped more of the tea, and as it sipped tea from its own mug.

"I'm having a hard time conceiving of what I am," I said.

"Well," it said, taking a long drink, "then it's a good thing that you're already you, isn't it? It's not really your job to conceive of yourself, for you've already been conceived. But you *can* know yourself, which is by far the easier of the two jobs."

With every drink I took, the creature seemed to gain solidity. Then I realized what was really happening: it was not really gaining solidity, but rather the room around it was losing solidity, becoming more liquid.

I looked down at the tea in my hands. "What is this?"

"Do you mean to ask what it is symbolically, metaphorically, metaphysically? It is a great many things, that cup. Most importantly, I'd say, it is a symbolic representation. I've given you something that I've prepared for you, and you are ingesting it. It shows a degree of trust, it shows the willingness for us both to have this dialogue, wherever it may lead, and the cup is an expression of myself I've offered to you, like you taking my hand to see where I might lead you."

The room's lack of solidity rolled in waves towards me, slipping up my legs and over my body. I felt it unlock my skin like a million tiny locks, and I leaned back in the chair as my body let go of itself.

"The only thing you can lose," hummed the creature across from me, "is what you are not."

I drank the last of my tea and set the mug on the table. The room was radiant – as if the wooden walls were made of thin sheets with hundreds of candles behind them, making them glow and flicker. Across from me Inconsequential looked similar, like candles shined softly through its form.

It finished the tea and set the mug down. I couldn't think of the person across from me as male or female, but it seemed as both at once. Or neither. With the strangeness of their form, any defining features were lost. Even the voice was melodious and light, not the gruff voice of some of the others. It looked at me with eyes that swam to and fro, each eye looking at me from a different place inside the rippling body.

I felt Em's memories losing their grip on me, or maybe it was my grip on them. Something stirred inside of my swimming body. I looked down at my rippling form full of golds and blacks, and I too was glowing from within. Then a small bubbling fountain rose from my chest, out into the space before me. I remembered it happening before, but I was the old W. I also remembered it happening to me as Em, that time in the coffee shop when I as Em drew symbols onto the refrigerator. Then those memories were swept away. Across from me a fountain bubbled up from the body of Inconsequential, curling through the air between us. The fountains from both of us met over the table, both of them lit from within. When they touched I felt an overwhelming vulnerability, something I'd felt when the old W had given over to Em, trusting her completely. I had also felt it as Em when her heart had been torn apart by her father, and when she'd tried so hard to talk to her mother about everything and her mother had shut her out. The vulnerability was too much.

I gripped onto the chair and squirmed away, the fountain pulling back towards me.

"Aren't you tired of that?" asked Inconsequential.

I closed my eyes, indistinct memories fluttering before me like falling tree leaves. "Tired?"

"Tired of bowing to feelings that are no longer relevant to you."

When I turned and looked back at Em, it was like looking at a sea of candles. "I don't think I can do this. I don't even know what it is we're doing."

"She wants answers," hummed Inconsequential.

I looked back at him.

"I can only tell her so much through that body sitting at the desk," he hummed. "What we're having here is the real conversation. The reason she came here. She's ready, and so are you. But she needs you to realize that you're ready."

I took a deep breath and relaxed a little.

"The fear you're feeling," sang Inconsequential, "the vulnerability, it's not something to give in to. It's something for you to realize. Do you think that she, the world, can't affect you in any way she wants? Do you think you have some magical wall of protection? We're all completely vulnerable, all of the time." A smile floated across its face. "The only thing you're hiding yourself from is the truth of that vulnerability. That perfectly beautiful nakedness. All armor is illusory – merely a weak collection of ideas."

I swallowed, feeling the taste of the tea lingering on my tongue. Closing my eyes again, I felt Em sitting behind me, felt her nodding. I turned to look back at her, and there was a thin stream linking me to her – a river floating in the air, moving back and forth between us. All of the other Inconsequentials were moving about the room, slowly, except for the most solid of them sitting in the chair talking to her.

Then she turned to me. But at the same time she kept looking forward. Part of her was talking to Inconsequential, and part of her was looking at me. In those eyes I saw the hidden part of her, the one who had created this form I was in, the one who had killed the old W. "I trust you," she said.

"But I don't know what to do."

"I trust you, as you've trusted me, and I'm asking you to trust yourself."

I took a deep breath. "I will try."

"Fuck trying," she said. "Just trust. Trust and do."

I nodded, then turned away from her. The fear was still there, but I realized that there was no confusion in me of what to do. So I relaxed into the chair and the fountain bubbled into the air once more, meeting with the fountain of Inconsequential. They bubbled into each other, and then my vision flashed and I was no longer sitting in the chair – I was standing at the edge of an underground river, surrounded by a long, rocky cavern.

The river was the life of this being called Inconsequential, all the things he'd done and all the people he'd communed with over so many years. I crouched down and dipped my hand into the water, and then the river and I became each other.

# chapter 27

One moment I was sitting across the desk from Inconsequential, the next I was in the house I'd lived in with my mom and dad, before my mom and I moved. I floated in the middle of the pristine white living room watching my mom clean. She didn't look particularly happy or upset, just neutral like always – like she had a job to do, and she'd display a pleasant demeanor while performing it, because the demeanor was just another aspect of the job. She dusted and vacuumed around me, and I knew that she couldn't see me. I knew that my dad was at work, and that I would be at school.

Then I realized that I wasn't really me – the eyes I was looking through were someone else's. I looked down at my hands and they were white satin sheets, billowing like sheets on a clothesline in the warm spring wind.

Everything in the room was white or pale blue or gray. No color too intrusive, no color too demanding of one's attention. As I looked into her, I felt my heart linked to her. I shook my head. "No," I whispered. Suddenly I knew that I was looking through the eyes of her extension. But how could she possibly have an extension? She'd buried anything artistic long before I ever knew her. Buried it, or maybe outright killed it.

"You can't have an extension," I said, and she turned off the vacuum and looked around, looked through me like she'd done so many times when I'd lived with her. She looked around the room slowly, as if searching for something she'd lost. That was when I realized that she was not one piece, one body, but many torn out pieces pasted together, like a collage made of torn-up magazine images.

Floating up to her, I gazed into her right cheek, where I saw a large man throwing furniture across a dark room, screaming like he was possessed. In her chin I saw a teenage-girl version of her, looking into a bathroom mirror with mascara streaked down her face, her eyes so completely lost yet incredibly determined. In her forehead I saw her sitting on the floor, a half-empty bottle of whiskey next to her, burning a picture of herself in a gown next to a man I'd never seen who was wearing a tuxedo. I almost didn't recognize her in the burning picture, because she looked so very happy. In her left eye I saw her as a little girl, pulling her crying little sister out of a second-story bedroom window and out onto the roof in the middle of the night, while yells and screams erupted from back inside the house. In her right eye I saw her lying in a hospital bed holding a baby, staring at the ceiling and quietly crying. Her crying eyes were locked doors, and I knew that she was crying for her own lack of feeling.

I shuddered. "Oh mom!" I cried, then embraced her. "I'm sorry. I'm sorry, I didn't know. I tried so hard to get inside, but you wouldn't let me."

When I opened my eyes, I was sitting across the desk from Inconsequential, my face soaked with tears. He was writing something on a sheet of paper, then he looked up at me and set his pen down.

"Can I get to the roof?" I asked.

He nodded, got up and walked over to the window. "I'll leave the window unlocked," he said as he slid it open.

I climbed up a ladder that led from the fire escape up to the roof. I sat down, leaning back against the short wall that bordered the roof, the sun warming my wet cheeks. I pulled out my phone and made a call.

It rang and rang, then someone picked up.

"Hello?"

"Mom," I said, nearly choking over my words. "How are you doing?"

"Em? What's wrong? Are you OK? Are you sick?"

"Mom, I just want to say that I'm sorry. I'm sorry for everything mean that I've ever said to you. I... I had no right to say anything like that to you."

"Em, I'm not upset with you about anything. You don't need to apologize."

"No, I do. I do need to apologize. And I'm sorry."

"Em, what's going on? Where are you?"

I felt a pressure inside my chest, as if my heart was being squeezed and rung out like a wet rag. "Mom," I said, sniffing. "I forgive you. I forgive you for everything. And I love you."

"Em. You're really scaring me. Tell me what's going on."

"I just really needed to tell you that." The pressure loosened in my chest, and my body leaned limp against the wall. I tilted my head back and felt the sun drying my face, making my cheeks sticky with dried tears. "Nothing's wrong, I just wanted to talk to you for a minute. I just needed to tell you that."

"Tell me you're safe," she whispered.

"I'm safe," I said, sniffing. "I'm going to send you some pictures of the artwork I've been working on. You don't have to like it, but I want you to see it."

"I'd love that. I'm sure I'll love it."

I took a deep breath. "I'm going to go now. I'm glad I talked to you."

"Call me again soon," she said, still obviously worried.

"I will. I love you, mom."

"I love you too, Emily."

\*     \*     \*

For the rest of the afternoon I felt lighter than I had in a long time, but also drained, like I was the walking dead. I left downtown without saying much else to Inconsequential. I knew I'd be seeing him again. I took the bus back home, drank a cup of tea and passed out for a few hours.

When I woke up it was dark, and the new W was there, sitting down and leaning back against the wall. The long jagged strips of him grew towards the ceiling. I walked to the kitchen sink and got myself a glass of water. "I want to start painting tomorrow night," I said, my voice still hoarse.

He nodded, barely glancing at me with his weird ashen eyes. I drank a couple glasses of water, then took a shower and left to go meet Red for a drink.

chapter 28.

Like a pillar I held up the wall and the ceiling. Like a guard stationed from the beginnings of time to guard the door to all, I was determined, I was still. The dark world of Em's room was so silent, broken only by the gentle metallic whir of the space heater. Her breath snaked through the air as she lay there asleep, carrying with it the scents of coffee, alcohol and sugar. I could wait a day, if that was what she wished of me. I could keep myself bound inside the body she'd encased me in, keeping those energies locked up for a short while. Those energies, which were really pieces of her that yearned to connect to her through the illusion of me.

Looking up, I watched the molecules of the ceiling spread open so that I could move through them. I would go and explore – it was too torturous to be in the same room as her all night and have to stay so separate.

Then she stirred on her mattress. Her shadowy silhouette sat up, framed by the streetlight coming through the curtain behind her. Turning to me, her eyes were wet glass in the near dark. She crawled out onto the floor, a slow and elegant creature, and somehow the shadows would not leave her even when she passed through the light.

"Em?" I said.

She slowly rose, and it was indeed her as she approached, still wrapped in shadow. She lowered her forehead against my chest and pressed her open hands to my shoulders. Her breath against my chest stirred my skin, making it ripple. The golden leaves which lay flat against my skin peeled away, stretching out as if to suck heat out of the air.

Her hands moved over my shoulders and chest, brushing through the golden foliage sprouting from me, moving the shadowy pieces of me around like cloth. She grabbed two handfuls of my shadowed skin and pushed me back against the wall, then pulled me and fell with me to the floor. My slivers of golden leaves and shadow whipped and writhed out across the bedroom floor, crawling up the walls around us. The leaves twisted and reached into the air, the shadows of me growing up in columns like trees, the leaves sprouting wildly from their tops to cover the ceiling. Pieces of me stretched outward, pulling me thinner and thinner beneath her until I covered the entire floor of the bedroom and had no trace of body left for her to hold onto. She stood up, and I saw her from so many angles at once, able to see from all parts of myself which surrounded her shadow-covered body. With her glassy eyes she looked down at what had been my ashen head, which was now a small white-gray puddle in the black forest floor. The leaves glowed dark gold. She knelt down, dipped two fingers into the pool of me, then drew two white-gray lines down one side of her shadow face. She then drew two dots onto her forehead, and three lines across the other side of her face. Em dipped her fingers in once more, drawing a line down the center of her body, starting at her chin. Leaning forward like she was bowing to the puddle, she dipped both hands into it. Bringing her dripping hands up, she ran them through her hair until most of it was ash-white.

She stood up then, looked up and around at all of me, at the forest of me. She walked up to a black tree trunk and wiped her hands on it until they were almost all shadow again.

And then she ran. The ground of me was bumpy and full of golden foliage, but she ran through it without tripping – jumping over large patches of golden leaves and ducking under shadowy branches. I kept thinking she would run into one of the walls of her room, but she just kept running and I kept being all around her as trees and foliage and ground. No matter how far I looked, I could not see an end to me – only her and myself in any direction, like a hall of mirrors.

She jumped and grabbed onto a branch of me, then pulled herself up into the canopy, climbing and pushing her way through golden leaves to get higher. Crouched in the branches, she pressed one hand against the black trunk of me and used the other hand to pry off pieces of shadowed bark, after which she crawled into the hole she'd made in the hollow tree, crawling inside of me. My bark skin closed around her, healing itself, and she curled into a ball. I wrapped tightly around her, holding her, saw the ashen marks on her face and the ash in her hair glowing in the midst of the dark inside me.

I held her there as she drifted off to sleep.

# chapter 29

I went to work the next day for the first time in I don't know how long. I'd woken up late, washed the gray off my face, but no matter how many times I washed my hair I couldn't get the white-gray out of it. So I dressed accordingly, wearing a gray and black hooded sweatshirt I'd made and a green skirt covered in black patches.

It was an afternoon shift in the middle of the week, so it wasn't too busy. Several of the regulars complimented my hair, and when asked how I'd gotten it that way I'd either joke about blacking out or say I dipped my head in ashes, not telling anyone the truth: that I had no freaking clue, except that I knew W was involved.

Halfway through my shift Matt came in. I was on the espresso bar and made his medium latte.

"Hi Em," he said when I handed it to him.

"*Gutten tag,*" I said. "*Wie geht's?*"

He smirked, but I could see he was uncomfortable. "I was wondering if we could talk. Maybe on your break?"

I started making the next customer's drink. "I think that could be arranged." Calling upon my barista powers, I steamed the milk absurdly loud, the high-pitched squeal ensuring that he couldn't keep talking to me. He nodded, went off to his corner and set up his laptop.

Half an hour later I told Meesha I was going on break and sat down across from Matt, setting a fresh latte next to his laptop.

"Thanks," he said. He shuffled through his bag and pulled out a book and handed it to me. "I got something for you." It was a book on the artwork of Gustav Klimt.

"Thanks?" I said. The cover showed a piece I'd never seen before, a giant golden tree with spiraling branches. To the right of the tree were two lovers embracing, similar to Klimt's most famous piece, *The Kiss*, and to the left of the tree was a jealous woman glaring at them. I flipped it open to see the name of the painting on the cover: *The Tree of Life*. "Thank you, Matt. I love Klimt."

"I know. I overheard you telling a coworker about him once when you were making drinks."

Hmm. Kinda creepy, but I wasn't gonna tell him so because he just gave me a gift. I glanced back to make sure there wasn't a line at the counter, but really I was hiding my face because I didn't know how to react. I'd never gotten a gift from a guy, at least not something that I'd actually want.

"You caught me on a good day," I said, looking back at him. "If you'd given this to me a couple days ago I might have lit it on fire."

"Oh." His eyes flicked from me to the laptop and back. "I haven't seen you here this week. Were you sick or something?"

"No, I've been painting. Well, that and I've been dealing with a lot of shit in my head for the past couple weeks." I glanced at the book. "I'm sorry I called you a coward, Matt. And Inconsequential shouldn't have said it either."

"I *am* a coward." His green eyes were tiny windows into a forest world. "I was wondering if you'd want to hang out, get a drink or something, some time this week. If you don't want to, I understand. I haven't been able to stop thinking about you and wishing that I wasn't so scared of –"

"Ope!" I raised my hand to get him to stop talking. "You've said enough. No need to make me think you're creepier than I already do."

"You think I'm creepy?" He looked genuinely hurt.

"I think you're awkward, and sometimes that awkwardness comes out in the form of creepy. Just like my awkwardness comes out in the form of bitch. But you don't think I'm a bitch, do you?"

He raised an eyebrow. "No."

"Good answer. Better than being honest." I pulled out my cell phone. "What's your phone number?"

I entered his number into my phone and called him. "Now you've got mine. Congratulations, I think we just graduated from acquaintance to whatever comes between acquaintance and friend."

"I don't know that there is anything between acquaintance and friend."

"There is. It might not have a name, but there's no denying that it's there, and that it defines what we are now." I picked up the book. "I should get back. Does tomorrow work for you?"

"Tomorrow's good. I like your hair like that, by the way."

I smirked, then leaned close to him and lowered my voice. "Do you ever black out and wake up with weird stuff lying around, or things painted onto your body?"

He sipped his latte. "You mean like waking up with gray hair?"

"Yeah, or with piles of gold-painted leaves on the floor of your bedroom?"

"No. But maybe I clean them up as part of my black outs."

I nodded and leaned back. "Maybe. I work until five tomorrow, so I could meet up with you any time after that."

He shrugged. "I could pick you up after work."

"Oh, you have one of those car things. Weird. I don't ride in cars very often." I tongued the inside of my cheek. "Sure, you could pick me up here. Five-ish. And thanks for the book!"

I got up and went back to work.

"So you actually talk to that guy now?" Meesha gave one of her goofy smiles. "That's a quick jump."

"Um, it comes and goes." I started cleaning up behind the counter, getting ready for the shift change.

"I've always thought he was cute." She peeked over the espresso machine. "And I can tell he's a good kisser."

I laughed. "Meesha, what makes you think that?"

Her almond eyes narrowed to slivers. "I can tell these sorts of things," she said with an air of authority. "It's something I'm always right about."

"What about Luke?"

"Are you kidding? Horrible kisser. But he's adorable, so he gets away with it. I asked one of his ex-girlfriends about it one day, before I figured out that my kissing hunches were always right."

"Too bad you can't somehow use that to gamble. Make some dough with those hunches."

She shrugged as she wiped down one of the counters. "I'm not complaining. It comes in handy."

After my shift was over and I was walking out, I glanced across the room at Matt and waved. He nodded to me and waved, his head straddled by over-sized headphones, and went back to his laptop.

W appeared floating next to me on my walk home. It was a bit disturbing, the space next to me growing darker and darker until there was a person there.

"Did you see Om at The Cove today?" I asked.

"She stayed outside most of the time. She likes to stand on the tables, not moving, like she's communing with the wind or the sunlight or something."

"That's kinda weird."

"Not really. I talk to the wind and sunlight quite often. As well as buildings and trees. Your building really likes you, by the way. It keeps reminding me to tell you so, but I keep forgetting."

"That's nice of it to say. What kinds of things do the others say? The wind and sun and trees?"

He shrugged. "They say what they always say. It's more of an exchange of energy and movement than actual words. They're speaking right now if you listen."

I listened around. "All I hear are the cars driving by."

"Stop walking."

I stopped and looked at him. It didn't really occur to me to try to hide from the passing cars the fact that I was talking to an invisible person. If they even noticed me at all, it would just give them something more interesting than usual to talk about at the dinner table. It was refreshing how much less I was caring about what people thought of me.

"Close your eyes," he said, and I did. "Now feel the sunlight on your face."

The warmth on my face did feel good.

"It's conversing with your skin, giving itself to you. Your skin is taking pieces of the sunlight, like offerings, into itself and distributing them through your body like food. The sunlight itself is pulling at your skin, blurring the edges of your face until there is no distinct line between your face and the sunlight. That's one thing I learned on a much deeper level from Inconsequential yesterday: that a true conversation is not the exchange of words, but the swapping of selves. It is the blurring between two things until they are no longer completely separate. But these conversations are happening constantly. You are conversing with countless things all of the time, whether consciously or not."

When I opened my eyes I was smiling. "Thanks," I said, then started walking again. "Do they ever talk to you with words?"

"Sometimes."

"Hmm. Neat. So... at Inconsequential's shop, did you see his extension?"

W was silent for a moment. "I don't know how to answer that. I saw multiple aspects of him, and they said that they were all the same person. The one that I would say was his extension, if he has one, and if they are not all his extension, is an amorphous floating puddle of clown makeup and facial features and clown clothing."

"Sounds nauseating. And kinda Picasso."

"I think I almost threw up again looking at it."

"That green shit isn't coming up off my floor, by the way. You're gonna have to cough up some money for my security deposit, when I eventually move. You might have to get a part time job or something."

"I'll... talk to your floor. See if I can get it cleaned off."

I shrugged. "Or you could do that, I suppose."

When we got to my building I went into the convenience store, spending the tips I'd made on Stoli and Kahlua. Sadly, Abid wasn't working.

When I got inside my room, I tossed my shoulder bag onto my bed and started making a drink. I looked over at the new painting, the painting that had torn apart and remade my friend, and butterflies flew up the center of me. W was stretching his body like an athlete getting ready to run a race. Or a hunter getting ready to sprint after his prey. Or prey getting ready to outrun a hunter.

I took a long drink, then said to him, "Do your worst."

"Put on some music."

Pushing around a bunch of CD cases piled in a corner, I pulled out one I liked to paint to – a band called *Qntal* – and put it on.

The gentle chanting hummed its way across the room, following closely behind the beating of drums. A lady began singing over the top of the other sounds, a song in a forgotten language – a song much older than any structure in this city. The fist-sized flurries rolled in circles around each other, spiraling out from the speakers of the CD player and towards the walls.

Em took another drink of her concoction, then went to the blank canvases leaning against a wall. From behind her, I put my hands on her shoulders. I slid a hand down her arm to her hand, pushed it out and picked up one of the smaller canvases with both our hands. I led her over and placed it on the easel.

Moisture came from her gray-white hair, like a scent with no smell, and it moved through me like a drug. I flattened our hands against the blank canvas, and felt my hand conversing with the back of hers while her hand spoke with the canvas. My other hand was still on her shoulder, and she grabbed it with her free hand and pulled it down across her chest. My body loosened, opening up to wrap itself around her like a cloak. I thought of the night before when I was the forest and she had crawled inside of me. Fastening around her, I covered all but her head and neck in my shadow and golden leaves, which began stretching out again to breathe in the air of the room, to breathe in the chanting and drumming and ancient words.

The strips of me writhed outward from us like snakes underneath the rolling flurries and up the walls, one strip of me wrapping around her table of paint and dragging it towards us across the floor. Em reached out with her black and golden-leafed arms and began unscrewing the jars. We took a brush, dipped it into a jar of violet paint left over from the first W painting and began mixing it with other colors, lifting it into a more vibrant shade, pulling it out into the light.

Each movement she made, as she mixed paints and then moved her brush across the canvas, stirred up a reflexive movement in myself. In turn, my movement would create a reaction in her body, and it became like a dance. Back and forth our bodies reacted to each other, neither of us truly in control, yet neither of us lacking control. I felt our bodies becoming like one, shifting against each other, encased in one another, pressing each others' buttons and turning each others' dials.

The flurries rolled up our bodies, up the walls which were covered in my gold and black, up the easel and the canvas like stars falling upward, or white-hot ashes rising from a fire. Then they nudged the brush this way and that in our hands, altering the brush's course on the canvas, and they too became an aspect of the dance.

Our bodies carried out a dialogue as they slid against one another. They spoke through the warmth that passed back and forth between us, that warmth carrying messages of thought, a species of thought that was not constricted by words. I closed my eyes and felt our movements playing at one another. I was spread out, wrapped under and around everything in the room, so with every movement of ours everything shifted back and forth with us. When I opened my eyes I saw clusters of golden leaves bowing up and down, back and forth to each motion of our bodies.

I looked over the top of Em's head, then slid one of my hands over her eyes. Her movements stuttered.

*Don't stop*, my body whispered to her body, keeping the dance going.

*I can't see*, her body said against mine.

*Use me*, my body said. *My eyes are yours. Feel me, know me. Use my eyes, and use me.*

The movements of our bodies were slow, but they grew steady and confident. I felt her behind my eyes, looking out through me like I'd looked through her eyes when I was inside one of her memories. Then, as her movements became more fluid and reflexive, I felt her breathing through my mouth, tasting the air through my lips. I felt her fear in my heart, fear of the way I saw the world, fear of the flurries rolling up the wall and easel, rolling up our bodies. But the fear was another reaction, another aspect of the dance, and it integrated into the movement of us, the movement of the room and the flurries and the leaves.

Our movement engulfed all that was around us, drawing into it every object of the room, the brush and the canvas becoming less and less important. No, not quite – the brush and canvas did not lose any value, but rather everything else in the room, and the room itself, gained immense importance. Every aspect of the room came to meet us, to converse with us, to move and to react with us. Like a crew sailing through a storm: the movement of each crew member in reaction to the movements of the boat; the boat moving in reaction to each crew member as well as the ocean and the wind.

The energy of the dance shifted and morphed. Sometimes Em and I seemed the hub of the energy, and it radiated out from us. Other times the energy seemed to be coming from the walls and the objects in the room, batting us about like a windstorm. Still, other times the energy seemed to come from the flurries and the music, nudging us this way and that. Yet no matter how the energy shifted, the movement would not stop, and the dance went on.

It seemed that this was our reality from now on: one long, endless dance. There was not a single thought anywhere in the room of the past – neither the past of Em, nor the past of the building or of the piece. Neither was there a future of any kind – only the constant promise of movement, movement that had never begun and would never end.

Yet it did end, and rather suddenly. Em was left standing there, the brush at her side and me wrapped around her. There was such a sense of finality, as if we'd just completed what we were created to do. As if this canvas, now soaked with color, was the sole reason for us meeting each other. But the canvas looked so pale compared to what we'd just done. What Em and I had just experienced was nothing like the act of painting, or the act of creation. The canvas before us was like the desert floor, showing our footsteps – where we'd been, how forcefully we'd moved, so that the future observer might get some brief glimpse, some nearly imperceptible snapshot of what had occurred on this night of nights.

Em shivered and I slid off of her, my body gathering itself back together. She picked up her knife, cut off a thin clump of her hair, and dipped it into her bright red paint. Then she signed the canvas, small, in the corner: W.

"Why?" I whispered.

Her eyes didn't leave the canvas. "Because W means both of

us. And we both did this."

The room began to lighten.

"The sun is stealing me away from you," I said.

She turned to me and her eyes were loud and alive, like two lions pacing. "Maybe it's you who steals the sun away from me. And now you're leaving so that I can have it back for a while."

My body was losing its grip on the objects it still held onto, like it was losing some of its solidity. "If I was able to hide the sun, and if doing so helped me be with you continuously, we'd both never see the sun again."

"Then you can tell the sun how lucky it is, the next time you two chit-chat."

I smiled at her. "Until tonight, Em."

"Until tonight."

# chapter 31

The night air was crisp and cool when I walked out of the pizzeria and onto the tiny cobblestone street, but my body was all warm from wine and gourmet pizza. I could smell the trees and plants from the nearby arboretum, and opera played faintly from behind me in the restaurant.

I slid my hands into the pockets of my hooded sweatshirt and looked up at the curl of moon in the sky as Matt walked up next to me. He followed my gaze. "We should get a better look at the moon," he said.

His green eyes were all glassy and glowing in the neon lights of the pizzeria. I couldn't put my finger on it, but I saw something like myself in him just then.

He looked at me. "I mean... if you'd like to."

I shook my head. "That was the first truly confident thing you've said to me, so how could I refuse? Lead the way."

We walked to his car, which looked more or less like every other car. A Toyota or Mazda or something. He put on some music when we got in – something slow and noisy with nice bass beat – and started driving us through the city.

"It all looks so different from inside a car," I said.

He seemed to think for a minute. "I suppose it would look strange to me from a bicycle."

"Do you own a bike?"

"No."

We drove on in silence for a few minutes. But it wasn't an awkward silence – it was just that he was a quiet person. The silence between us felt alright. We'd talked quite a bit at the restaurant – about our families, where we'd gone to school, where we'd grown up, all that first-conversation stuff. Of course I'd left out the bad parts about my dad, just said he was in jail and that I might tell him about it some day.

"This isn't *your* music, is it, Matt?" I asked him.

"No, I hope someday I'm this good. This CD is a compilation of musical projects by this guy I really like named Bill Laswell. He does all sorts of collaborations with different people – Iggy Pop, Jah Wobble, The Golden Palominos."

He glanced over at me and I shrugged. "I know who Iggy Pop is."

"Bill Laswell's got a pretty big underground following. This track coming up is by his group called Material, from this album where William S. Burroughs does spoken word. The album's all about Egyptian mythology – death and the different parts of the soul."

"Well, I like it so far." Then the raspy and wise voice of William S. Burrows began spilling over the layers of noise and beats. I couldn't quite make out all of what he was saying. It's always hard for me to recognize lyrics on the first listen. "And I know who William S. Burroughs is too, of course."

We were driving past all the empty business parks, the streets getting more and more empty around us.

"Who's your favorite performer?" he asked.

"Ugh. That's one of the worst questions. No one worth talking to about music has a favorite band. I bet you don't have one."

"I always do, but it switches every couple of weeks."

"So what you're really asking is, who's my favorite this week?"

"Sure."

I twisted my mouth and thought for a moment. "Probably Bessie Smith. I've been pretty hooked on her recently. Nothing quite like someone who can make you smile while they're singing about their woes."

He pulled into an empty parking lot, then into a parking garage.

"Is this the one where we saw Inconsequential?" I asked.

"Same one."

We drove up to the roof and he parked. He opened his door. "Shall we?" he asked.

The moon was a sliver of diamond in the star-filled sky. The wind was colder up on the roof, and I hugged myself to keep warm as I stood looking at the sky.

Matt opened his trunk. "Here, I've got an extra jacket," he said, taking a long coat and draping it over my shoulders like a cape.

"Thanks, Matt."

He quickly stepped back, like he suddenly realized that he was touching my shoulders. He ran a hand through his messy hair and smiled. "Sure."

I looked past him at some milk crates full of things sitting in his trunk. "What's all that?"

"I brought my music, in case you wanted to hear me play."

"Of course I do! You want to play *here*?"

He shrugged. "This *is* my studio."

"Well, ok then."

"It takes a little bit to set up." He began pulling out the crates.

"Need any help?"

"No, I've got it."

I wandered over to the wall where I'd watched Inconsequential. The other rooftop was so empty and dark and normal-looking. I saw W out of the corner of my eye, but didn't look at him. We'd decided not to let Matt or Om know that I could see W all night now, rather than just at twilight. I'd probably tell Matt eventually, but wanted to figure him out more first. Who knew if Matt would get all weird and upset and just walk off?

I closed my eyes and pictured the cool wind communicating with my face, the way W had shown me. This strange life had become so normal to me now. I didn't know what I'd do if everything suddenly went back to the way it had been – or if that were even possible.

After a while I walked back over to Matt, who had a small card table set up with some electronic gadgets, including his laptop and some speakers. He had two short plastic boxes like cut-down milk crates which each held a dozen wine glasses in place, each glass with a different level of water in it. Wires were running in and out of these boxes, and I could see small microphones attached to the glasses. His trunk was full of crumpled newspaper that the glasses had been wrapped in, and there were a bunch of empty plastic jugs that had been full of water.

He was fiddling with some switches on one of the gadgets. "Just about ready." His huge headphones hung around his neck, and he pulled a bottle of wine from his trunk. "Would you care for some?"

"Sure."

He opened the bottle and we both took a drink from the neck. "I have wine glasses, but unfortunately they're all in use at the moment."

"Sometimes glasses just get in the way."

"That's what I figured." He took a deep breath and looked at me. "I've never actually played for anyone. My heart's racing."

"Relax. Just enjoy it."

He took one more drink and handed me the bottle. His eyes glossed over and he began nodding his head and tapping his foot to some beat I couldn't hear. He wet his fingers in a jar of water, then moved them along the rim of one of the glasses, creating a long, deep humming sound. He stopped, then did the same thing over again, and then flipped some switches. The humming sound began repeating through the speakers. Matt wet the fingers of his other hand and created two more notes that crawled atop the first note. These notes were higher, lighter.

My own heart began to stir in my chest. I wasn't sure if I'd ever heard anything so peaceful. He kept layering notes upon one another, notes which were pulled into his laptop and looped, pumped back out the speakers over and over, repeating into the air around us slowly and methodically. I felt my body vibrating from the noise, and my whole mood was swayed by their whim. It sounded like a chorus of voices, and I suddenly realized where Om had gotten her name. "Om" was the sound that some of them made.

Then he began playing a tune over the top of the repeating song, and it was so sad and quiet and lovely. His head leaned against the headphones on his shoulder, his eyes half closed, his body swaying with the music. I knew then that I was hearing something that no one had heard before – I was experiencing something new. He looked so peaceful, his hands moved quickly over the tops of the wine glasses – like his body was the slower, methodical beat and his hands were the playful, quicker melody. Like I was hearing different emotions vocalized by water and vibration.

I thought I saw the air shimmer above him, and wondered if I'd glimpsed Om working with him. *Of course it was Om,* I thought to myself as the song went on. *There's no other way for this to happen.*

The song was like a story, and it was obvious when the story was over. The quicker melody trailed off and ended, then one by one as he tapped and turned the dials and switches the other layers faded out, until only the first, deep humming remained.

"God," I said. "That was completely amazing."

"Thanks." He looked up at me like we'd never met, and I realized that I was seeing a deeper part of him – he was made up of many parts just like I was. I handed him the wine, and he took it like it was a foreign object, then smiled as if suddenly remembering what it was. He took a couple of drinks and handed it back, his green eyes blazing in the dim light.

"I've got another one," he said.

"I'll stay here all night."

He smirked, and he had that look again – the one that meant we both knew some incredible secret about the universe. *This* was the part of him that was giving me that look. That's why the rest of Matt was always confused by the way I acted – he hadn't even known he was looking at me that way.

The deep hum continued to vibrate out of the speakers. *Hummmmm. Hummmmm. Hummmmm.* Matt messed with his equipment and the humming sped up. He played his fingers across a wine glass, creating a high pitched note which also repeated, and the first hum quickened until it was like a drum beat. He played a slow song over the top of the beat, another peaceful melody, then all the noise stopped completely. He played one, lone note, which trailed off into silence. Then another lone note, which also trailed off. Then a cacophony of loud, slow beats erupted from the speakers – the humming drum beat that he'd made along with other more electronic sounds that must have been coming from his computer. He began playing melodies over the top, slow melodies that contrasted beautifully the loud booming and grinding of the electronic beats.

I couldn't stop myself from smiling. The music instilled me with energy, and there was no way I could just stand still. I took a swig of wine, set the bottle on the ground and began to dance. I let my body sway with the music, trying to dance to both the harsh, slow beat and the beautiful, serene melody at the same time. I saw him get more into the music, so I let myself get more into the dance. The beats moved and shifted underneath the melody – the melody floating over them like bees moving from flower to flower.

Eventually the music shifted, and I could tell that it was a different song. He'd begun a new song so that I could keep dancing. This one was more chaotic, the main beat quicker, and the melody he played with the wine glasses would quicken until it was nearly impossible to dance to, then slow down until you could nod your head to it, then it would quicken again. It made the song sound like it was breathing, like it had its own life force. I stopped dancing after a bit and watched him create. With this song his fingers were all over the tops of the wine glasses, barely ever having a chance to mess with the electronics. His eyes were half shut, but I could see them moving back and forth over the glasses.

Suddenly the music cut out and there was only the quick melody of the wine glasses. He slowed it down, adding in some bass notes, then ended the song.

I clapped and jumped up and down. "That was so fucking great!"

He leaned forward on the table, breathing heavily.

"You alright, Matt?" I asked.

He looked up and around at the sky. "You stay the hell away from me," he whispered, though I knew he wasn't talking to me.

I picked up the bottle of wine. "That was incredible."

"It wasn't supposed to cut out like that. Om fucks with my electronics sometimes, especially when I play a couple of my more electronic songs in a row. I don't usually, but you were dancing and I got inspired."

"Well, I had a blast, even if Om didn't. Thank you so much." I handed him the bottle. "You look like you could use some of this."

"Thanks." He took a deep breath, smiled a little, and took a drink.

"You're lucky. I think painting for me is like making music is for you, but I don't think people would be very interested in watching me paint. Especially since it takes me somewhere between eight hours and a few months. So all I can do is show them my paintings."

He walked around the table and pointed to the concrete railing. "Feel like sitting down?"

We walked over, climbed up onto the stone railing and sat down. "I don't know," he said, handing me the wine. "At least when you're done with a painting, you're done. You don't have to keep painting it for people over and over again. You get to constantly create something new."

"I guess so. I've just been realizing that no one will ever know my true art form, they'll never know what happens when I create.

Like what Jackson Pollock used to say. He thought the creation of the painting was the art, and the painting was just what was left. He didn't know why people wanted to buy his paintings."

He leaned back and looked up at the stars. "I could really agree with that. So do you think Jackson Pollock had an extension?"

"I have no freaking idea." I looked at his face, which was paler than usual from the moonlight. I was trying to figure out how much to tell him, but then I figured that I'd asked him to be himself and not think so much about what he was saying, so I should be natural too. "To tell the truth, I've started to think that everyone has an extension. Just that not all of them manifest."

He shook his head. "I don't think they do. The soccer moms and cheerleaders and lawyers. They're not like us."

"I don't know, maybe they don't all have extensions." I looked up at the moon, the broken diamond. "But I like to think they do. Or that they have the potential to have them."

Neither one of us spoke for a moment, then Matt broke the silence. "You know, in Japan they don't have the man in the moon. Instead of seeing a face up there, they see a rabbit making rice cakes."

I laughed. "What are you talking about?"

He smiled. "You can't see it now, but look up when the moon is full and you'll see. Ever since I learned about it when I was taking Japanese, I can't see the face in the moon anymore. Only the rabbit making rice cakes."

I handed him the wine. "You're pretty funny."

"Most people don't think so."

"Well, most people aren't as cool as I am. They're not privy to the secret knowledge of who's funny and who's not."

"Then I guess it's lucky I met you." He took a drink.

"Everyone who's met me is pretty lucky to have met me."

He laughed.

"You should laugh more," I said. "It suits you."

Matt looked at me, and I could tell that part of him wanted to look away but that he wouldn't let himself. "Ok, I'll give that a try."

# chapter 32

The wind pulled at me, stretching me out into the night. I sat crouched atop a water tower on the roof of the building where Em and Matt were eating dinner. My hand touched the rusted metal of the water tower, the age reaching into the black and gold of my skin, like a million tiny hands reaching into mine to hold on to me, if just for a moment. The night felt alive and feral, and I would not wander far from Em while the night was in such a mood, or when I knew that Om was near.

"W?" whispered a voice near my ear. I spun around and stood up. I had to trick my eyes into forgetting the night so that I could see the nearly invisible extension.

"Hello, Om."

She floated there, her infinite starry eyes looking into me. "What's happened to you? You're entirely different."

The air was thick with the smell of her fear and vulnerability. What the other W had done to her while defending Em had changed her, scarred her. Her voice was lacking the utter confidence and superiority she'd had when they had first met.

"I was destroyed and then remade," I said. "By Em."

"Destroyed? Why would she do such a thing? How is that possible?"

I crouched back down, the golden and black trails of me dripping down like a curtain and nearly covering the water tower. In that moment I realized that Om was no longer much of a danger to Em or myself, so I did not feel like I needed to keep secrets from her. Though I still would not leave her alone with Em. "We'd gone as far as we could go together, with the state I was in. I'd fulfilled my purpose, and Em fulfilled hers by dismantling me and reforming me into a new state, with a new, deeper and more complicated purpose."

She drifted closer to me. "I do not understand. Why would she need to dismantle you? And why would you submit to such a thing?" Then, as an afterthought she added, "I do not mean any kind of insult by these questions. I truly want to know."

"I cannot explain why. It was just what needed to be done. I knew she was going to do it, and I asked her to. As for submitting, she is my creator. I would do anything within my power that she asks of me."

She was silent for a moment. "It is strange how differently we see things, W."

"I don't think so. Our makers are very different from each other."

"W..."

I stood up. "They're leaving."

We followed them through the air, trailing behind and above the boy's car. When we reached the parking garage, I perched upon the small building that housed the elevator and the door to the stairwell. Om floated up next to me.

"You were saying something," I said.

"W... Matt did not create me. I was borne of sound, and over time I grew more layered, more complex. I was a host of vibrations all braided together, and I took some of the vibrations running through me, spinning them together like a spider, and I created a being that would move through this world, connect with this world, and create new vibrations for me and out of me. I did not see a way to fully interact with the world as I am, so I created Matt as a conduit."

"How long has Matt existed, then?"

"Time is like a sound – it is not real. It's like a thought, or something written down on a piece of paper – you can kind of see it, but it has no real value. It can be changed on a whim. It's a sound that comes and goes, but has no real substance beyond that vibration – like a mirage. Sometimes you can hear it and it is there, and sometimes it vanishes for a while, until the note is played again."

Across from us Em and Matt got out of the car. He put a coat over her shoulders.

"If Matt's whole past is fabricated by you," I said, "then is the rest of the world real?"

"Of course. The world is made up of vibrations, and they are very real. But Matt is the only thing in this world that I've created."

"And who made you?"

"I don't know my creator," she said, and I could hear a gentle sadness in her voice. "But I'd like to think that they are as protective over me as I am over Matt, and that they do not wish to be seen by me."

\*          \*          \*

As Matt began setting up his table and his tools, Om moved behind him and emitted a long, beautiful note that stretched out from her chest and into the air – thin, twisting tendrils in the air between them. Matt stopped preparing his equipment and stretched, arcing his body as the tendrils of sound pressed into the small of his back. His arms stretched out as the tendrils moved into and out of him, all across his back and down his arms. He flexed his hands and stretched his neck, then bent forward again and continued preparing his tools, the tendrils flowing through him and glowing green in the night.

When he began to play, Om moved in a slow sort of dance, her movements foreshadowing his own, like a wave moving from her through the tendrils and into him. From the speakers the white flurries poured, but instead of rolling across the parking garage roof, they floated out into the sky, corkscrewing through the air, around Matt and Em and the table. The circles they made grew wider and higher, and then they would dive down into Om where they disappeared, recycling themselves back into her movements to be reborn through the speakers, again and again.

Em started to dance, and I could feel her body pulling at me. I slipped behind her, my energy merging with hers as we moved as one. The shreds of me rose up into the air like an inverted tornado above us, twisting in the midst of the circling flurries.

Suddenly Om yanked herself from Matt, the tendrils of sound recoiling back into her. She plucked one of the flurries from the air and blew it into one of the electronic boxes and the beats coming from the speakers stopped. The flurries in the air drifted out into the sky like untethered balloons or kites or paper lanterns, and the smaller ones coming from the wine glasses rolled off the table onto the parking garage roof instead of floating into the air.

Matt yelled, "You stay the hell away from me!"

Om's starry eyes were furious. "We have a deal," she muttered, though he could not see nor hear her.

She floated up to me. "I need to leave, W. I'll talk with him about this at dawn."

"I'd like to talk to you more," I told her.

"Some other time," she said, and dispersed into the wind.

# chapter 33

"You *sure* you don't need another hand?" I called down the stairs.

"No room for another hand!" yelled Luke. "We got it!"

I pulled my door completely open and started kicking my clothes and junk out of the way. Luke and Red came in, carrying the big, twisted blue-green steel frame with the equally big mirror mounted at an angle to the bottom of it.

"The hooks are over here," I said, leading them over to where I'd installed some large metal hooks to mount the frame. "Just a second, let me get the painting in." I picked up the first W painting and fit it into the back of the frame right-side-up (according to how I painted it) and twisted the little levers that Red had installed in the frame to keep the painting in place. "Alright, it's good. Now up on the hooks."

"Maybe we should have thought this through more," grunted Luke, his face tense and strained.

"Thinking never got me anywhere," said Red as they hefted it up onto the hooks and let it go. "'Sides, there's more satisfaction when you just up and do something and it actually works."

Luke rubbed his red-lined hands together. "Whatever you say... holy crap!" He was looking at the painting. He backed up and nearly tripped over some of my clothes.

"It's the shit, huh?" said Red.

"Em... wow... I don't know what to say."

"Thanks," I said. The metal of the frame twisted out like thorns or jagged waves around the piece, like the frame was alive. I inspected the angle of the mirror, how it captured enough of the piece, even while looking at it from different angles, to give the effect of the piece upside down. "It really works." I shivered, suddenly realizing that I was looking at the image of a dead friend in the mirror. "It works..."

"That is... this is really something," said Luke.

"Glad you think so," said Red. "'Cause I'm enlisting you to help convince Jacob to let us put Em's work up in The Cove, and to have an art opening."

"What?" I said. "What art opening?"

"Oh yeah, I came up with that yesterday. We'll give out wine, have a band or two. It'll be great!" Red poked Luke in the chest. "Your band should play."

Luke shrugged. "I'm sure they'd be up for that. Especially if there's wine."

Red turned back to me. "You said you were on a roll creating smaller pieces, right?"

I nodded. The idea was starting to sink in more. "If we do this, you've got to do frames for all of them." She was already nodding. "But the other ones won't need mirrors, unless you think they need them. With the frames, each piece will be two pieces of art combined and I won't feel like the show's all about me."

"Deal," said Red.

"And I *might* be able to get Matt to play at the opening, too. You guys would love his music, but he's super shy, so I don't know if he will."

"Wait," said Luke. "The boyfriend guy? Go Emster!" He raised a hand to give me a high five but all he got was my middle finger.

"Let me see the others," said Red.

I hung the gold and black one back up next to the framed one. "This one won't really need a frame, since it's got the diamond. But maybe something behind it, coming out from the edges?" I handed her the three pieces I'd created with W over the last couple of weeks. All three of them were twelve inches by twelve inches.

"How many do you think you could make in the next month?"

I shrugged. "At least a few. I was going to try to make a tall one next."

"Just keep the dimensions coming," she said.

Luke was staring at the new W piece. "Holy crap, are these real leaves?"

"She doesn't know," said Red. "Her alter ego did that part. Like Clark Kent and fucking Superman. Or maybe more like Jekyll and Hyde."

"Hey Em, can I get your alter ego's phone number?" asked Luke.

"It's a guy," said Red. "But he *is* pretty hot."

"Hmm... probably better not then," said Luke. "I think my old lady would kill me if I went on a date with a guy. Especially if he was in someone's head." He took out his cell phone and checked the time. "Speaking of the dame, I'd better take off. We've got a movie date tonight."

"Anything good?" I asked.

Luke shrugged. "This week it's foreign film, which is her department. German, I think. Next week it's horror week, though. I wrote up a list of movies and can't figure out which one we should see. I'm weighing the pros and cons of trying to convince her to see five horror movies over five days."

"Good luck with that," said Red. She turned to me. "I guess I'm catching a ride back with him."

"Thanks for helping us bring the frame over," I told Luke.

After hugging them both goodbye, I sat on the floor across from the two paintings now on my wall. But they weren't just paintings, they were three-dimensional.

Pulling out my cell phone, I called Matt.

"Hi Em," he answered.

"Hey Matt. I had a lot of fun the other night."

"Good." His voice sounded a little shaky and I bit my lip. "I really liked hanging out with you, and playing for you. I had a long talk with Om, and I don't think she'll do that again. At least not if you're there."

"So I had a question for you. You know how I told you that me and Red were going to convince our boss to let us put up my paintings?"

"I remember."

"Well, now it's becoming this big thing. We're pretty sure we can get him to let us do it, and I'm going to make more paintings and Red's making these bad ass frames for them. And we're going to see if he'll let us have an art opening. We'll make fliers and have wine and bands."

"That sounds great!"

"I was wondering if you'd play for my art opening."

"I... I don't really do that, Em. I mean, I might some day, but..."

"You don't have to say yes, but maybe you could think about

it? I thought this would be easier than a concert, because people won't just be there to see you. You'll be part of an event, so there will be other things going on. And you could just play a few songs if you want. Luke's band will play, so it's not like you have to play for very long. They've got tons of songs."

"Em, I really don't know."

"Well, will you think about it? Even if you just consider it, it will mean a lot to me. I mean, I really like your music. And it would go so well with my paintings."

"Alright," he said after a moment. "I'll think about it."

I smiled and leaned my head back against my wall. "Thanks, Matt!"

"Sure. Now I have a question for you. Have you ever heard of the band CocoRosie?"

"I've heard their name around, but I don't think I've listened to them."

"They're sisters, and their music is really pretty and experimental. They're playing next week, and I was wondering if you wanted to go. I really think you'll like them."

"Yes! I mean, wait. Let me think about it." I paused. "Yes, yes, after pondering the idea, weighing the pros and cons, I think I would like to accompany you on this endeavor."

Matt laughed. "Cool. Maybe we can get dinner before."

"Maybe," I said, then switched to my evil villain voice. "*Maybe indeed.*"

Every day I followed her out into her world, and every night she followed me back into mine, where the creation happened. Sometimes what we made was new, and sometimes we picked up threads we had dropped the night before, but the dance was never the same. It was always fresh, always unique. My body changed with the energy pouring from me. I looked mostly the same, but I could feel the changes inside. The constant flow of energy I channeled into Em was altering me. Like a river coursing over rocks for so many decades that it made them smooth, the energy channeling through me was smoothing out anything in its way until its movement was no longer hindered at all. My body was becoming a clear channel, an instrument, a flute. And inside I felt nothing but joy and a total sense of purpose.

Em continued to work during most days, and sometimes to go and see Red. She even went and had lunch with Matt a couple of times. The smaller paintings began to multiply, and she would take them over to Red's house to fit them into frames. But the pictures of the old W and I she kept on her wall.

My body began to tire and wear thin during the day, and sometimes I didn't go with Em when she left. I would sit silently on the roof top, communing with the wind and the sun and the clouds. I even began to sleep a little, dreaming of the most wondrous creations.

On the night of the concert, Em busied herself in front of the mirror – something I hadn't seen her do before. She painted her face a little with makeup, making her eyes and lips darker, and pushed around her black and gray hair. She pulled a black and green dress from the back of her closet. Memories came to me – memories of being her and constructing the dress from a green Indian-print sheet which had small dark green and yellow elephants marching across it amidst patterns of curling vines and leaves. After she pulled on the dress, she went back in front of the mirror and added a black vine which curled out from the corner of one eye, a vine that matched the ones on the dress.

"I want you to come," she told me from inside the bathroom.

"I'll go if you wish." I was up against the wall, communing with all its pieces, and all those pieces' pieces.

"I think it'll be good for you to just chill out and listen to some live music. We'll both take the night off. And Om should be there, right? You two are on good terms now. You might be able to get some social time in."

I liked the idea of talking to Om, yet at the same time I didn't know if I wanted to spend my energy talking to her. Energy was something I no longer had an excess of.

A strange impulse made itself known to me – an impulse to not let Em go alone. It was not my impulse, but one that belonged to the old W. It was one of the pieces that made me up, and it showed me his view of Em being a frail creature in a chaotic and stormy world. The impulse had no hold on me – like the vague memory of a dream – and I was going to go to the concert because Em asked me to. But then I was filled with a sudden nostalgia for the old W – perhaps because he could not feel that nostalgia for himself. And instead of going for Em, which was the real reason, I changed my mind and went in honor of my predecessor, without whom I would not exist.

                    *          *          *

The cool night wind unrolled long, thin golden strands of me out over several buildings as I crouched atop the large advertisement billboard, which depicted someone holding a can of soda and smiling uncomfortably. Looking down at the parking lot of Chicken Karma, the Indian restaurant that Em and Matt had gone into, I sensed Om approach me from behind.

I had a little more energy, perhaps on loan to me by the cool night air.

"I wasn't sure that I was going to come along," she said.

"Me neither."

"I'm glad you did."

I turned and looked at her, and the clouds unfurling across the sky like great gray carpets made it easier to see her glittering star-eyes, floating amidst the strong winds and twinkling buildings in the distance. She seemed tired, but I thought I could be projecting my own exhaustion onto her.

Gesturing for her to join me, I felt the the billboards' lights humming against my hands and feet. The galaxies in her eyes were slowly turning, and I could see some of the tiny stars exploding into great flashes of violet and blue.

"My note," she said. "The note of me is ending, W. The strum of the string is over, and I can feel the sound of it, the vibration, fading out. I can feel myself ending."

I nodded. "Have you told Matt?"

She shook her head. "I don't know how to tell him, or even what it means."

"Sounds like you think too much."

After a moment, she answered: "Perhaps I do. But I feel a terrible responsibility for Matt. I wove him out of vibrations, and without me playing his tune, he will fade away. And we're not done yet. We're not finished here."

My eyes passed over the sea of rooftops, the clouds above us darkening and just beginning to rumble. The air was so charged, and my body greedily sucked up the electricity from the air around us as well as surging through the billboard underneath me. I hesitated, not knowing if I should be the one to help her. For one, this was all between her and Matt, or her and herself. Also, what advice could I offer? I hadn't been around for long. But I imagined myself in her position, and knew that I would welcome any well-intentioned opinions.

"What if Matt plays your tune?" I asked.

"I told you, he does not."

"I know, but what if you taught him to? Your creator, as you said, played your tune and you are playing Matt's tune. Now your creator has stopped playing your tune, so what if you could teach Matt to play it before you fade out? Then you would be sustaining each other. Or you would be sustaining yourself through Matt."

"That... seems unnatural," she said, shaking her head. "Almost perverted."

I shrugged, feeling the electricity spinning my atoms, sending them knocking into each other like the balls of a pool table. "As Em would say: *fuck it*. Why were you created? Why did your creator create you? So that you can wither and die before you're finished doing what you were created to do? I've died once, Om, and I will most likely die again. But when it happens, I will know that it is the only way. I will *want* it. If your creator has instilled in you a will to stay alive, then it seems the unnatural and perverted action for you to take is to not act on that that will, to not do everything in your power to stay alive."

Several more stars in her eyes were exploding, silent in those ovals of universe. "I don't know how any of that would work, but I will consider your words, and perhaps I will find a way."

I stood up, body-memories of Em flooding through my arms and body. "Fuck trying, Om!" I grabbed her shoulders (which felt like great gushes of wind) and peered into the vastness of her eyes, not caring if vertigo sent me falling from atop the billboard. "What do you desire? What is it that drives you right now?"

"To be with Matt," she said hesitantly. "To explore this world with him. To create."

"And why do you have that desire? Where does it come from?"

"It's in me," she said, touching her chest. "It's part of the vibration of me. It is me."

"Yes," I said, smiling. "So is it perverted to follow that desire? To follow the desire that makes you up?"

"I think you're right."

I shook my head. "It has nothing to do with me. And if I'm right, then it'll come to you. The knowledge of what to do with Matt, whether to teach him or to do something else entirely, will come. Because it will have been built in by your creator."

"How do you know all this?"

"Because I know Em" I glanced towards the restaurant down below. "Everything that I know flows to me from her. I have no knowledge of my own. I am an instrument, a pipe in her frail hands."

"Thank you, W."

"You're the one who's going to go face the challenges. Don't thank me – thank yourself for facing them. Thank yourself for doing the impossible."

# chapter 35

The lights flickered in the little Indian restaurant and my face burst into a smile. I wondered if it was pouring and thundering outside. Matt was wearing a dark blue button up shirt and black slacks, but his hair still had the messy claws-on-forehead look. The shirt didn't go as well with his green eyes as his corduroy jacket did, but he still looked handsome.

"You... you look amazing tonight," he said.

My face grew hot. "Thanks." I long drink of wine. His eyes had told me right away that he thought I looked amazing when he'd picked me up from my apartment, but it had taken roughly half an hour for his mouth to say so. I wanted to give him shit for not telling me sooner, but I'd promised myself I wouldn't be a bitch for the night. Or at least that I'd make an effort.

"Do... um..." he trailed off, adjusting the buttons of his shirt sleeve. Evidently he hadn't promised himself not to be awkward. At least he hadn't been creepy yet. "I was going to ask you about your paintings, but then realized that you might not want to talk about them."

"Yeah, not really. I could use a break from all that for the night. To be more precise, I could use a break from *me* for the night." I took another sip of wine and smiled at him. "So you've made it to date number two. Well, not including getting lunch."

"Is that rare?"

"Matt, it's a feat of Herculean proportion and will be written about in the song books for ages to come." I'd been asked out on plenty of dates since I started working at The Cove (not surprising – being a barrista raises your appearance rating by at least two), but I'd never felt so comfortable on them, and they rarely became second dates and never third. The only "real" relationships I'd had were both long distance, and both years ago while I was still in art school. Matt was the first person I'd been on a date with that seemed more like a colleague, someone on my level – and also weirdly like a brother, which I'd have to sort out in my head.

"I don't date very often either," said Matt.

I laughed. "I guessed as much. Sorry, I shouldn't laugh. I'm not laughing at you, I'm laughing 'cause you're like me."

He smiled. "Do you want to see how I started making music?"

"More than anything."

He licked his lips, then started moving the condiments from the side of the table and placing them between us. Holding a spoon and fork in one hand, he began tapping on the salt and pepper shakers, making different sounds against the glass while letting the silverware clack against each other. Then, dipping a finger into his glass of water, he began playing his wine glass.

My wine glass had a bit less wine in it, so I pushed it forward to give him another note. "You can play mine too," I whispered.

The tiny sounds he made on the condiments reminded me of a xylophone, and a boyish smile crawled across his face. It sounded like the soundtrack to a fairytale. He stopped as the waiter walked up with our food, which was full of curry and spices and smelled divine.

After the waiter walked off, I said, "That was magic."

"Thanks. I haven't done that in a long time. Its what I used to do when my parents took me out to dinner."

"Your parents must be pretty cool."

He shrugged, putting his napkin on his lap, which reminded me to do the same. "They're alright. They were always nice to me growing up, but they were the kind of parents who treat their kid like an adult. Which is good in many ways, but sometimes a kid just needs to be a kid. I think when they had me they realized that they didn't really want kids, so they didn't have any more." We both started on our dinner. "What about you? What are your parents like?"

I wrinkled my nose. "My parents aren't really good dinner conversation. Or date conversation. I know that's rude of me."

"I don't think its rude. Tonight is about enjoying ourselves. So we should talk about whatever we want."

"Good. Thanks." I marveled again at how comfortable I was with him and his aura of awkwardness. "You're a good guy, Matt."

He leaned forward and whispered, "Don't tell anyone."

I laughed. "Your secret's safe with me."

*          *          *

The venue for the concert was medium-sized and pretty packed, and we got a good standing spot near the center of the floor. There was a DJ on the stage mixing noisy, slow dance music.

"What do you want to drink?" Matt asked.

"I'll get this round," I said. "You've payed for everything."

"Let me, just for tonight. I want tonight to be my treat."

"Ok... Just tonight, though. I don't do well being doted on all the time. And thanks. Thanks for tonight, I'm having a really good time."

"It's my pleasure."

I glanced back towards the bar. "Hmm. What to drink. I usually do Black Russians, but I've been drinking them a lot while painting. What are you having?"

"I was going to get a Dark and Stormy."

"A what?" I laughed. "Did you just make that up?"

"No I didn't just *make it up*. Its dark rum and ginger beer with a lime."

"Ooh, ginger beer. And rum, huh? It could be a rum night. I'll try that."

Matt reached out and touched my elbow and a shiver ran up my spine. I hoped he didn't notice. Then he turned and was swallowed up by the crowd between us and the bar.

I held my elbow where he'd touched me, closed my eyes and took a deep breath. My elbow felt warm, and the rest of me suddenly felt cold. "Fuck," I whispered. "Chill the hell out, Em." I took some more deep breaths and kept myself calm, and was feeling normal again by the time Matt came back.

The lights dimmed just as he made his way back to our spot. Some of the crowd began cheering, and I tried the drink. "It's good!" I told him. "It totally passes the Em test."

"Good."

"And you're not doing so bad yourself."

"So I'm passing the Em test?"

I shrugged and smiled.

Two guys walked onto the stage then, one of them sitting at a keyboard and playing a very pretty piano melody on it. After a moment, the other one used a microphone and began to beat-box over the piano. Then two women came onto the stage, and the crowd began cheering for them.

One of them wore a gown and sat down at a harp, which she began to pluck. The other woman, wearing a tank top and some kind of military officer's cap, walked up to a microphone and started singing. Her singing was something between talking and singing, almost rapping. Then the song shifted and the woman at the harp stopped playing and began singing operatically with her arms in the air.

I was transfixed on them – the whole experience was so intoxicating. I felt like they were pulling music from nonexistent worlds and weaving them to life in this world. None of it sounded real – it was too beautiful, too magical to be made by four people on a stage. Four people that didn't look much older than I was.

For the second song the woman who was singing and rapping picked up a toy from a table right beside her. Then I realized that the table was covered in toys. She pressed buttons on it and it made animal sounds – a cat's meow, then a cow's moo. And somehow the sounds became more haunting than silly. They melded into the robotic beat-boxing and slow melodies of the keyboard. Then the other woman began playing some kind of flute I'd never seen before.

I looked at Matt and his green eyes were so intense and fixed on the stage, drinking up all the sights and sounds. He hadn't just taken me to a show, he'd taken me into his world – he was showing me a part of himself. Looking back at the stage, I leaned my head against his shoulder. Matt shifted uncomfortably, then put his arm around me.

I shivered a little and my whole body felt like it caught fire, but I didn't care. I just tried to keep breathing deep, and let the music reach into me, calming me with its serenity and its poetic, breathtaking tales.

Closing my eyes, I said without speaking, *Just give me this night. Just this night.*

chapter 36

I was electricity. The atoms that made me up flipped and hurled themselves in every direction, passing each other like infinite ghosts – not connecting, yet affecting each other with an intimacy only lovers could carry. Reacting to each other without touching – a sort of tango. How could I even know of such a dance, but through the memories that flood through me like sticky blood, like drug-infused smoke, creating whole worlds in my mind that may or may not hold any real truth?

"The last time I saw this group," Om said, "it altered me. Changed me."

"Talking to me has altered you," I told her. "Every experience alters you."

"I created Matt so that he could deal with these parts of the world," she said as we floated above the roof in the crashing, thunderous rain. The rain, which was uncertain whether to roll down my form or pass through me – in the end deciding to weave through my body, like worms crawling through the soil of me before coming out the other side and splattering against the rooftop.

Any other day of my experience I would have left her there, for what had I to gain from changing her mind? And how could I know what was best for her? But the storm had charged me with its energy, and I was not in the mood to leave things be. I felt ornery, and dealing with that electric mood brought a sense of life into me that I'd never felt.

"You told the old version of me," I said over the rain, "that you made Matt to experience the parts of the world that you were unable to experience – not so that you could use him as a shield. If you're better than Matt, a more advanced being like you say, then what could he casually experience that would be too much for you to handle?"

"I'm changing, W," she said, and I could hear sadness woven through her wind-voice. "We've been creating so many new songs, and we've been experimenting. Matt's been changing his style. Every time he stretches his methods, every time he changes techniques or uses something new to make noise, I grow. But it's not really growing – it's that I'm stretching out; I'm becoming so much thinner than I've ever been."

Then I saw it. I was used to pushing my eyes to see her, so I hadn't noticed that she was even more difficult to see than usual – less of her was visible.

"How does it make you feel?" I asked. I could feel the concert pulling at me. Om was right about one thing – something was going to happen inside the building below us.

"I feel alive, W. But also like I'm vanishing. I'm scared. Scared and alive."

I nodded. "It's ok to feel afraid. But if I were you, I wouldn't follow what makes you feel safe, because that's just listening to your fear, which is wrong. My fear has always been wrong. If I were you I would listen to what makes you feel more alive, whether it's going into this concert or not."

"If I get any more spread out, I think I might lose the cohesiveness of my thoughts and memories. I feel like the next time we meet, I might not remember you."

"And does that make you feel more alive?"

"Yes, W, it does."

I smiled at her. "I hope I see you inside. But if not, then sometime soon."

"Sometime soon."

I fell down and passed through the roof of the building and into the music venue. The room was large, dark and full of talking people. There was a man on the stage wearing headphones and weaving noise together to make music. After a few moments the music stopped and the lights dimmed.

The first two musicians walked onto the stage and began creating music as I hovered above Matt and Em, the black-streaked golden strips of me stretching out over high above the audience's heads. I sensed Om and saw her floating far behind me, a whisper of wind in the back of the room.

Then the two women took the stage and the world before me

shattered and split like a fanned deck of cards. Blue smoke poured across the stage, billowing up into the air around them and making images out of itself – figures and animals, sailing vessels and wings. The air between them was glittering and broken, like a fun house mirror that's been shattered, each shard showing a slightly different angle of the scene. The billowing blue smoke rose up, teasing the shifting shards. In both the smoke and in the shards I sensed an intelligence – there were six on stage rather than four.

One of the women played a harp as the broken shards of reality turned and spun like pieces of a wind chime. The blue smoke poured out over the crowd like an ocean as the other woman began singing or talking over the music. The little white flurries poured out of the speakers, quickly changing color and pulsing with rainbow light. The flurries bounced off each other, bounced atop the pillows of blue smoke like children jumping on a bed, bounced over the audience's bobbing heads.

As the smoke rolled over the audience and towards me, it was suddenly obvious why Om had not wanted to come in here, and why she was so afraid; why she was *right* to be afraid.

A drum was beating far away, slow, steady and loud, calling to me.

*Thoom.*

The essence of me shook as I watched the smoke draw nearer, the smoke which now sparkled with tiny shards of reality – countless shards, slowly turning like the shards on the stage.

*Thoom.*

Calling me, the drums. Fear riddled my body, and my words to Om came back to me. This was the line in the sand, this was where my words to her became words directed to myself, and where my words evolved into action.

*Thoom.*

I grinned at my fear, let it flood through me. Let the electricity burst and flicker inside me, let it dance with the fear, let it breathe life into me.

*Thoom.*

The woman at the harp stopped playing and raised her hands into the air. She looked right at me as she began singing long, drawn out operatic notes, her arms beckoning to me. She was only the third human to ever look at me, the only others being Em and Inconsequential. As she beckoned with her arms, voice and eyes, something inside of me answered. A fountain rose from my chest and out into the air between us. The fountain twisted and churned in the air, being pushed gently back and forth by her voice. The faraway drumming had stopped, and she stopped singing. She smiled at me and went back to playing the harp, and the other woman started singing as the music jerked into a louder existence, suddenly more layered, more ecstatic.

Seeing the musicians on the stage, I couldn't make out how many extensions there were. It almost seemed like the smoke was one and the shards of reality were another, but I couldn't be sure. And if they *were* two extensions, they were woven into each other. Then the cohesiveness of the scene dawned on me – the extension or extensions and all four musicians were one thing, moving as one unit, yet I could see that the movements were completely inspired – none of it was very rehearsed. The extensions affected the four musicians, and the four musicians affected the extensions.

The glittering smoke wafted up and over my legs, the shards of reality colliding with the electricity buzzing inside me. The fountain twisted in the air between me and the stage, weaving around through the beats and the woman's words.

The song faded and bled into a new one, and the whole scene altered drastically. The smoke became a colorful world adorned with oceans and land – trees, sky and clouds. The shards of reality spun and swallowed up the whole stage, leaving only the musicians standing in the new world. The words and music and beats pouring from them grew into strange creatures of all kinds.

My mind could not hold onto my beliefs; I could no longer fathom musicians and extensions – those ideas of reality wouldn't stick with what was happening before me. I was watching the creation of a world. Creatures spawned from the land and evolved over time, interacting in love and pleasure, in heartbreak and war. Time and space dissolved – I was dragged over countless centuries and miles. Words and song grew into stories of that world – the beats were the sounds of the world shifting and evolving.

The drum beat, far away, began once more, echoing across the lands of the world.

*Thoom.*

The creatures looked up to the sky, asking their leaders and medicine men what to make of the drumming.

*Thoom.*

The trees shook and stretched even higher in the sky. The clouds reached down to caress the trees' branches, like a lover apologizing for being gone so long.

*Thoom.*

The world flickered like the light of a candle against a wall, battling with the shadows.

There. Not there.

There. Not there.

*Thoom.*

The creatures and the trees and the plants were gone; only hard-packed earth remained under a darkening, cloudless sky. A fire burned, a small bonfire with a shadow sitting close and holding a drum. A shadow-hand came down on the stretched skin of the drum-head.

*Thoom.*

The shadow looked up at me and set the drum down. It motioned to a log on the other side of the fire. "Sit down at the fire with me," she said. Her voice sounded very old, and I was sure that it was not any version of Em I was looking at. "It's going to get cold soon."

I sat down.

"Are you an extension of one of those women?" I asked.

The shadow studied her hand. "Don't worry about how I define myself. It's more important for you to know how you define me, to know what I mean to you." The shadow smirked (which I may not have been able to see if I hadn't gotten so used to watching the subtleties of Om's movements). "I can be however much or little you want. Just as you can be however much or little I want."

Desert stretched out in every direction. The whole world was brimming with an alive lifelessness. "Where are we? At the end of that story? The story on the stage?"

"We're at the end of all stories. Or rather, beside them. We've stepped out of time, W."

"How do you know my name? I don't know yours."

"You *will* tell me your name, so you *have* told me your name. We're outside of time, outside of every conversation we've had or will have. You're used to time, so you're imagining that you're still experiencing it, pretending that there's a future that you haven't yet come to. But that's not really so important. The illusion of time is just an interesting tangent, really."

"What should I call you?"

"Oh, W," she said, laughing. "Even in your imagined time-world, we've spoken before."

Then I knew who she was – well, sort of. "You're the... world?"

She shrugged. "I can be, if that's what works for you right now. I can be an extension of one of those women, perhaps pretending to be the world, if you want. I can be the world pretending to be the extension of one of those women. I can be both of their extensions, or a conglomeration of every extension. I can be the only thing that exists, manifesting all of reality. Or I could be a figment of your imagination – or Em's imagination – nothing but a passing thought."

I nodded. "You said we were outside of time. Where are we?"

"We're beside the world, beside existence. A lot of beings would say the edge of the world, but its more like being before the world starts and after it ends and next to the middle, all at once. I like to think of this place as being right before the thought that starts the world."

"Why have you brought me here?"

The shadow full-on laughed. "*Brought* you here? For one, everyone's always here all the time, on some level of their being. You can't be brought here. For another, I was just playing my drum when you showed up and interrupted me (not that I'm complaining, I welcome your company). But you should be asking *yourself* why you've come here, not me."

"I don't feel like I chose to come here. If I did choose it, I really don't know why, except to experience something new."

"Not new. This is where you were when you chose to go into existence. This is where you were before you began and after you ended, and where you will be before you begin and after you end, and where you are while existence appears to be happening."

As she said the words I knew they were true. I'd been there before, beside the world, beside time. Suddenly I felt very comfortable, sitting there on that log looking over the fire at her. The sky darkened, and it was getting cold like she said it would.

"I am here to gain perspective," I said, and as I said it the words became true.

She nodded.

"Like a person swimming in a pool, studying objects at the bottom. I wanted to come up for air, to look down at the surface of the water to better see the position of the objects beneath me. So that when I go back in I have more perspective, and I can be clearer."

"Clearer about what?" she asked.

"About what I want. About my intentions."

"Interesting. And what do you intend?"

"I want to push Em. Push her further. And I want to die – I want to die again."

The shadow bowed her head.

"What do you want?" I asked. "Why are you here?"

"Me? I want to sit by the fire. To feel its warmth as the air grows cold. To say more than that would depend on what it is I am. If I am the world, then I want existence to be existence, I want to revel in all aspects of creation. If I am an extension of one of those women or of someone else, then perhaps I am like you, gaining perspective. If I am part of your or Em's subconscious, then I'm here to ask you questions, to help you clarify your intentions. If I am a being who has yet to choose which existence they will travel into, then I'm here to leaf through lives like the books on a bookshelf, figuring out which life I'd like to experience."

I stood up and stretched. The shadow was becoming harder to see as the sky darkened and the fire threw itself brightly over her blackness. "Thank you," I said. "Whoever or whatever you might be."

She smirked. "Have fun."

"I'll try to remember to do that."

She picked up her drum and brought her palm down on it.

*Thoom.*

Broken pieces of the concert came from every direction, spinning as they flew across the desert floor. The beats and noise and singing came to me like remembering a dream.

*Thoom.*

My body wrapped around me, as if I wasn't already in my body, becoming heavy and dense, my sense perceptions reaching out and drinking in sound and cool air and collective body heat and moisture and different colored lights and smells of alcohol and humans. The darkening desert and the fire disappeared behind the shards of the world, yet I could still feel them there behind everything, like a humming engine giving life to the experience around me.

The blue smoke was gone, and the shards of reality sealed together so that the cracks disappeared. One of the women was playing some sort of electronic toy, and she glanced up at me and tossed me a ball of black shadow covered in tiny diamonds. It flew up towards me and then exploded like a bomb, the blackness and diamonds wrapping around me and becoming the night sky. The electricity inside me burst from my body, zapping all the tiny diamonds, which were amplifying the electricity and sending it back into me. It was too much, so much energy everywhere. I crashed down into the crowd, landing between people, and saw the electricity and diamonds overlaid atop everything. I stood and moved through the audience and towards Em, determined and half-blind. I needed an outlet – I needed release, and now.

"W, are you alright?" said the wind in my ear.

I turned and saw Om in the crowd behind me, and the gold and black strips of me, riddled with lightning, brushed across her. She reeled back as the lightning crawled all over her form. "Om!" I yelled, but the closer I got, the more lightning jumped onto her. I turned and pushed through the crowd to get closer to Em, the diamonds continually enhancing the electricity running through and around me.

Em was there with Matt's arm around her, and I reached out. I tried calling her name but the only thing that came from my mouth were sparks of lightning. My hand finally touched her back and the electricity gushed out of me and into her.

But the diamonds were reflecting so much back, magnifying it faster than I could pour it into Em. I needed to release more. I screamed mouthfuls of lightning, sparks bursting from my eyes. My whole body lit up, shivering into and out of existence, and I felt again the edge of the world, there just behind everything else. As I reached into that feeling, that place, the walls of my body became less substantial and the electricity flew out of me in every direction, into the entirety of the crowd. I felt their molecules flipping and dancing, so charged with electrical current. I felt their vibrational frequencies rising the faster their molecules flipped, matching the levels of the people on stage. The energy pouring from me in waves was chaotic, unchecked and dynamic, but the diamonds were modifying that energy, stabilizing it before it flowed into the audience. Soon the whole room – the audience, the music, the performers and the extensions – were vibrating at the same frequency, all except for me, as my own frequency was jumping all over the place.

Then the diamonds went to work on me, and I felt the jumping levels inside start to even out, start to harmonize with the rest of the room. Suddenly all the energy became waves – waves that poured out of me, through the diamonds and into the crowd. Then the energy would bounce off the walls of the room, flow back through everyone, back through the diamonds and into me. Wave after wave after wave. I stood up straighter. Em was in front of me, still next to Matt with her eyes fixed on the stage, though I could see the tiny sparks of electricity jumping from her body into the air around her.

The musicians were still on stage weaving their music together, stories unfolding around them in the air like holograms that shifted texture when one song merged into another. The woman who had been playing the harp jumped up and down, dancing like a young girl. She locked eyes with me, pressed her hands together like she was praying and bowed her head to me. I pressed my electrified hands together in the same way, and then bowed back to her.

The stage was like an island, with waves moving from me and crashing upon its shore, then moving back to me, into me.

# chapter 37

Creative energy surged up through me like twin whirlwinds. I was in awe. The performers pulled at my emotions, dragging them out in the air between us, their words shaping my creativity like glassblowers shaping searing hot glass with their breath. So many images flashed across my mind – ideas on how to push the limits of my painting, how to fine tune some of my techniques, how to expand on some of the concepts that I liked to work with. I'd never seen a show that moved me so much.

The concert went on, each song and combination of instruments more interesting than the last. I don't know how long the drumming was there, but I didn't notice it until an hour into the concert. Coming from nowhere, it was distant and slow, and the more I heard it the more I felt a vast and growing discomfort in my body – a growing sensation of wanting to take my skin off, to ditch my body like a cocoon.

There were too many people around me. I was surrounded by bodies and music and emotion, and it was too much. I needed space around me. I felt sweaty and gross and cold.

Matt's arm tightened around my shoulder, and he tilted his head over. "This song's one of my favorites. And they always perform it differently."

Each word he said came packed with images.

Image: My dad putting his arm around me. "Want to get a burger, Emily?" he asked. "We can pick up a cross-eyed puzzle on the way."

"*You're* a cross-eyed puzzle," I heard my little girl voice say.

"You kiss your mother with that mouth?"

My little girl voice laughed.

Image: The framed photo of me and my mom and dad, up on

our entertainment center. We were all smiling, looking so very family-ish.

Image: The other photo we took, where me and dad made funny faces but mom wouldn't. She still had her fake smiling face on while we looked silly. She would always hide that photo, and every few months dad would find it and switch it out with the normal one on the entertainment center, and if I noticed it before mom hid it again I'd lose my shit laughing.

Image: My dad being escorted into the courthouse. My mom didn't let me testify, not wanting to put me through that. He had pleaded guilty anyway, so there was nothing my testimony would have done. I snuck out and took the bus on one of the many court days, traveling across the city to the courthouse to watch him enter from across the plaza. He wore a cheap-looking suit and was handcuffed. It had been several months, and he looked skeletal with sunken eyes and his hair slicked back. When I saw him there, walking up the steps, every doubt of whether he was guilty was erased from my mind. What I saw wasn't a man – it was something half-man, half-monster – and the man-part knew that the monster-part had finally destroyed his life.

Image after image after image: Dreams and dreams where my dad would keep being nice and hugging me, and I couldn't get away, like he emitted a gravitational pull that surpassed the earth's.

I pushed away Matt's arm and shoved my way back towards the front entrances.

"Em, you ok?" he said, keeping up with me and putting a hand on my shoulder.

"I need to go," I said, not sure if he could hear.

Shoving my way through the sea of people, I thought they'd never end. I was so hot, and the people all around were stealing my breath, and my lungs were fighting to pull it back from them. I was going to start screaming. Then I pushed through the first set of doors and into the room with the ticket booth.

"Are you feeling sick?" Matt called after me.

I pushed through the glass doors and when the cold night air hit me I sucked it in. It had stopped raining, and the ground was covered in puddles. I walked up to the curb, leaned against a small tree and raised my hand to a taxi, but it had a fare already and kept going.

"Em, what the hell's going on? Are you alright?"

I turned to him and tried to say something, but my voice broke and I started crying. "I can't be something I'm not. That's what the fuck's going on, Matt." The tears that fell down my face made me hate myself even more. I never let anyone see me cry, ever. "Take a good fucking look, 'cause this is who I am. This is what I do."

I flagged down another taxi and this time it pulled over.

"Don't take a taxi, Em. I'll take you home. You left your jacket inside."

I got in the cab and shut the door.

chapter 38

I knew Em and Matt had left the concert, not by my connection to her, but by the change in the vibrational frequency of the room. But I had too much energy flowing into and out of me to merely float away – the electricity bound me like glowing chains – so I focused the energy flowing through me downward towards the floor, and it shot me up through the ceiling, the burst of energy sending people away from me in waves.

Once the cold air hit me, I felt the excess electricity leaping off my skin and out into the air. I was so high up, almost at the clouds, and I hurled myself back down towards the music venue and saw Em getting into a taxi. Flitttering down upon it, I grabbed onto the "TAXI" sign sticking out of its roof and held on as it sped down the streets. The air felt good against me, and my body felt hollow and moist without all the excess energy flowing through me. It felt good.

When we arrived at Em's apartment, I flew up and passed through the wall and into her room. When she entered she was crying. She made herself a drink, half spilling it on the counter.

"Em," I said.

"Shut up! Just shut up! I need to be alone! Or at least pretend that I am!"

She spilled the rest of her drink on the counter, then cursed. She stomped over and yanked on her bookshelf until it tipped over crashing onto the floor. Walking over the back of the bookshelf, she fell into a crouch atop her mattress, staring down at the sheets. "Fuck you," she whispered. "Fuck you for making me this way. I shouldn't have to live like this. This isn't mine." She wiped her nose with the back of her hand. "I shouldn't be this way. You shouldn't have done this to me. You had no right."

I wanted to put my hands on her back, to wrap myself around

her and comfort her, to hold her and tell her that everything would be alright. Really, I wanted to tell her that everything *was* alright. Maybe if I touched her, opened up the connection between us, I could absorb some of those memories and emotions – and maybe lessen their effect on her. But I heeded her wish and let her be.

She stayed that way for some time, and eventually crawled into a ball and fell asleep.

I thought that we might not create for a while, and the thought of it scared me. I still had some of the electrical energy coursing through me, and I didn't know what I would do if she didn't want to create.

But the next day she went to The Cove, and that night she came home and made herself one of her drinks. She seemed a little tired, but not sad at all. "Let's get started," she said. That night more than the previous nights I nearly vanished, and we created until the sky outside began to lighten.

"Damn it," she said, when she saw light falling through the window. "I don't feel like stopping yet."

"We can keep going. You don't need to see me for us to create."

She shook her head. "I like feeling you there with me when I paint."

I touched her shoulder. "You can talk to me about what's bothering you, if it helps." I did not tell her that I already knew. That every night when we came together it was like dipping my face into a pool of her thoughts, her memories. But I did not know if she was aware of all the things that I saw.

Her voice was dry and scratched when she spoke. "I have no words," she said, looking right into my eyes. She nodded around to all the paintings. "These are my words. These are what I speak with. What I scream with."

Over the next several nights we kept painting, kept creating. Em would sleep at dawn, but she slept less and less as the days went on. At night her phone would start making noise – she'd look at it and turn it off. We were so close, her and I, and I knew who was trying to reach her. I felt him in her mind when we began to create, felt her use the energy of us to push thoughts of Matt aside. Like a river pushing things aside that impeded its flow. Like a river smoothing out rocks.

I became as thin as paper. The forces flowing from me into Em each night had worn me down to a kind of utter simplicity, pulling me closer to transparency. I no longer had the energy during the day to conceptualize the world, or to dream up meanings to my and Em's shared existence, or even to access Em's memories. Yet I was content, for as I was pulled thin, so was the world. More and more I felt and sensed the edge of the world. As I was being hollowed out of concepts, so too was the universe around me. It grew simpler alongside me, and it became content along with me during the daylight while Em was away.

Sometimes I dreamed, but my dreams bled into colors and feelings, and eventually my dreams were just two-dimensional images stripped from my past or from Em's past. Images that had nothing behind them, holding no meaning. Like when the first W came into existence, how all he could see of Em's memories were images that he couldn't fathom. When she killed him and created me with pieces of him, I could access her memories at a whim, yet now those memories were once again flat and almost meaningless, weathered away by the river.

I breathed deeply, and each breath was a long conversation with the world of Em's bedroom, which I hardly left anymore. I would sit there leaning against the wall, sometimes underneath the two paintings, sometimes across from them so that I could look at them. My energy was so low that I conserved it in every way I could, in order to have as much as possible for the dance each night. Sometimes I would see the edge of the world in Em's walls. Like all those molecules had been the entirety of the world the whole time, hiding and pretending to be the walls of Em's bedroom. They would smile at me and I would smile back.

"You're asking the right question now," they would tell me. "You're asking it with your whole being."

# chapter 39

Every time I walked into work, my stomach would cramp up when I glanced around to see if Matt was there. He hadn't been to The Cove since the night of the concert, which was over a week ago. I knew I'd have to talk to him soon, but every time I tried to fit him or my feelings into my head I felt like they were much larger than I was. Like there was a building crashing down on me and I'd somehow frozen time, and my survival depended on thinking of a way to get out from underneath the building. I'd been hoping that waiting would help me see things clearly, but all it did was help me realize how mucked up things were inside.

Meesha was working, and I was glad. She was so normal in her own quirky way, and knew less about me than most of my other coworkers. She also didn't usually mind taking up register duty when I wasn't in the mood to deal with customers, letting me hide behind the espresso machine. Luckily it was busy enough for the hours to blur by as Meesha sang each drink to me operatically and I kept churning out the drinks through the afternoon.

During one of the few lulls, I took a break outside, drinking a double espresso and staring at my phone. I couldn't bear the thought of talking to Matt, hearing his voice. I knew that was beyond what I could handle. So I texted him, writing out the whole words in an attempt not to sound silly:

Sorry for what happened. Kinda crazy right now, trying to sort stuff out. I'll call when I'm more normal-feeling. And I'm really, really sorry. I understand if you hate me.

I stared at the words. Then I deleted the last sentence, thinking it sounded too petty and sad, then hit *send* and shut my eyes, letting my thoughts and fear drown in the noise of the people eating and chatting, of the birds hopping around and chirping while searching for crumbs underneath the tables. "Fuck me," I whispered. Taking a deep breath, I got up and went back inside.

*          *          *

Towards the end of my shift, when the closers were due to come in, Red showed up. It hadn't really occurred to me that I hadn't seen her since before the concert debacle.

She walked behind the counter with a hand inside her leather jacket. "Sup, sweet-cheeks," she said.

I smirked, when normally I would have laughed. "Not much. Did you pick up the closing shift?"

"Nope. I'm here with strictly devilish intent." She leaned forward and whispered, "Crime."

"Sounds exciting."

"Oh, it is!" She pulled her jacket open to reveal that her hidden hand was in the shape of a gun. "It's a kidnapping. And you're the target. If you say anything to anyone, I'll pop everyone in this joint."

"You got enough bullets to do that?"

"I always carry extra clips."

I sighed. "Red, I don't think I can. I'm in the middle of this piece, and –"

"Shht! I said kidnapping! How many kidnappers do you know of that go around asking who wants to be kidnapped? Huh? None that are any good!" She looked around to make sure no one was listening. "Now, in ten minutes when your shift is over, you're gonna walk out of here nonchalantly and all, and I'm gonna follow. Try to run, and I'll wing you. And then you'll be kidnapped and wounded, which is much worse! So don't do it!"

All I wanted to do was go home and paint and drink, which was all I'd been wanting to do since the concert. It had become stupidly obvious that I wasn't making any progress sorting shit out in my head while on that current routine, but feeling the progression of myself through my art gave me a sense of accomplishment – and I needed that right now. That, in its way, was keeping me sane.

But it had been too long since I'd hung out with Red without just dropping paintings off to her, and I knew there was no way out of it.

"Alright," I said. "I relent."

"Good, glad you see things my way."

"*Red is here,*" sang Meesha, coming out of the back room. "*Red, Red, Red, dressed in leather, hand in her jacket.*"

Red peered over her shoulder and whispered, "She knows too much."

\*         \*         \*

I stretched my arms and leaned back against the brick wall of Red's building, looking out towards the sunset peaking over all the triangle rooftops and scattered trees. We sat on the catwalk outside her window, drinking cans of Highlife and sharing a cigar.

I'd been uncertain about the whole not-painting endeavor, but as the beer and tobacco circulated in my system I began to relax more, to ease into my present circumstances. Closing my eyes, I felt the last of the sunlight communicating with my skin, felt the cold increase as the volume knob on the world's temperature was turned down. Soon I'd have to pull my jacket tighter around me, but not yet.

On the way over I'd been telling Red about all my pieces, about how looking back at them they seemed to tell a story about the W's, showing their births and evolutions and deaths, and even the way they both related to each other. I wasn't sure if anyone else would sense anything like that, though. Of course she knew I was avoiding talking about Matt, but it wasn't until we were on the catwalk that she mentioned him.

"So you've been painting a lot, that's good," she said. "But that's not all, right? You been all over that new boy of yours too, I'm sure. How's that going? Is it all starry-eyes and groping and poetry? Is he still annoying, or did he drop that?"

I took a swig of beer.

"Uh oh," she said, seeing the look on my face. "I still got my gun and my clips. I can take him out."

"I... uh." I looked at her, but my eyes just started tearing up. I crawled over and hugged her, pressing my face into her shoulder.

"Hey girl," she said, wrapping her arms around me. "Em? What the fuck's going on? Did he do something to you?"

I shook my head. "No. He didn't do anything."

"Oh, Em," she said, and I could tell she knew suddenly what had happened to me. Hearing that realization in her voice made me feel so good, and like a dam being blown open I just began sobbing and sobbing.

"It's ok, girl," she said. "I'm here."

*          *          *

After a while I stopped crying. I went inside, splashed water onto my face in the pitch black bathroom/dark room, then went back onto the catwalk. I leaned back against the bricks and drank from my beer, which was warm now.

"I needed that," I said. "I feel better than I've felt all week."

"Good to hear. Then I won't tell you how you look."

I smirked and flipped her off.

"So when was the last time you saw him?" she asked.

"The concert. It was really good – all of it was – the band, Matt, the whole night was perfect. It was too good. I just had to fuck it up and flip out."

"Did you hit him or scream at him or anything?" asked Red.

"Not really. I just ran away."

"Have you called him?"

"I texted him today. Just said I was sorry and that I'd call when my head was straight. But I probably scared him off anyway."

Red shrugged. "Maybe, maybe not. Seems to me you need to figure out what you really want with him. I mean, sure you gotta sort things out in your head and your heart, but you can tell him that. If you want to be with him, you can say sorry and that you hope he waits for you. If he likes you enough then he'll say yes, and if he doesn't he'll say no. And if he says no, that just makes it a little easier for you."

I already knew everything she was saying, but hearing her say it made it all sound so black and white, so simple and obvious. "Yeah, that makes sense."

"As for that bastard who's supposedly your dad, take it from personal experience – that shit's not going anywhere. It's inside, and it'll stay there. If you keep pushing it away, it'll keep ruining your life. You just gotta figure out how to kick it in the balls, put it in its place and make peace with it the best you can. Like saying to it, *I know you're not going anywhere, so I built you a little house in a pretty little forest in my head. You can live there for the rest of my life, and if you wander out of your little area, I'm gonna kick your ass and put you back.* And you might have to go and visit it there, in that house. Just go there every so often and hear what it has to say. Otherwise you're ignoring it too much, and things might get bad again. 'Cause remember, it's not actually your dad in your head. That thing that you hate is a piece of you. And in reality, it didn't ask to be that way – it didn't ask to be the fucked-up piece of you. It thought it was supposed to be a normal piece, like you thought you were supposed to be a normal girl. So you and the fucked-up piece have a bit in common, if you think about it."

"How in the hell do you know all this? I mean, I know things were crazy with your dad, but you never even went to counseling. I've been to counseling and I've never heard it put that way."

Red shook her head and puffed on the cigar. "Trial and error, my friend. I'm only a year older than you, but my dad started screwing me up quite a few years before yours did, so I've got some experience to top you."

We sat there, watching the last of the sun's rays disappear behind the buildings. I was getting pretty cold, but felt so much better. I still ached inside and my stomach felt like an acid pit, but none the less it was better.

"My last piece of advice," said Red. "Talk to Matt. Tell him in person what you want from him, no matter what you decide. 'Cause even if you don't want to date him, you obviously get along with him and you two should keep hanging out. And no matter how much you tell him that his friendship matters to you, if you tell him on the phone it's gonna come off being half-assed or fake. And do it soon, like tonight or tomorrow."

I started tapping the back of my head against the brick wall. "My stomach is knotting back up just thinking about that."

"Well, just figure out what you want with him. Don't think about the talking part."

"That's the problem – I know what I want from him. I just don't know if my head will stop being crazy."

"Then follow what you want, even if he has to wait a while. And if he doesn't wait, then it wasn't meant to be. And don't worry too much about what you'll say. I find it's best in these kinds of situations not to plan it out. Just trick yourself. Pull out your phone and call him to meet up, before you know what you're doing. Then you won't sound rehearsed."

"Or I just won't say anything. Or my words will fall all over each other."

Red shrugged. "It happens with us humans. I don't think he'd hold that against you."

chapter 40

The walls were humming with the impacts of the bouncing pale flurries that collided against them. Each of the little creatures was about fist sized, and they traveled the wooden floor of the bedroom like wild packs of buffalo, like flocks of pigeons across the sky. It was day and Em had left a window open for me, but the sky was overcast and it was still dim in the room.

Wondering where Em was, I searched through my memories as I sat against a wall. There were so many memories to choose from – she'd left me in her room countless times now. Going to hang out with Red, going to work, going to the park to relax or to sketch, going up to the roof. I wasn't sure which of the memories had taken place that morning (she couldn't see me during the day, of course, but she always told me where she was going anyway). The only memory that was obviously from the night before was when I had asked Em to leave her stereo on the next time she left. I didn't know what type of music was playing, but the slow, methodical drumming reminded me of the drumming I'd heard at the concert. Sometimes a woman sang or spoke poetry, and sometimes there was just drumming and the deep thrumming of a stringed instrument.

The flurries moved to and fro in packs, in slow spirals across the floor. The patterns they made were both organic and like the churning of gears inside a machine. I felt a tug at my leg and looked down to see one of them pulling at me. Without eyes it looked up at me, pleading.

"I would join you," I said, "but I can't. The little energy I have left I need to save for Em." I smiled down at the creature, and my dry lips cracked a little, tiny gray shards of them raining down onto the flurry who quickly shook them off like a dog shaking off water. My whole body was dry and on the verge of cracking, and it seemed to be worse during the day. One of the roaming packs of flurries spiraled close to me and a few of them collided against my leg, bouncing off of me and leaving a few divots haloed by cracks in my skin. I felt the divots being made, but there was absolutely no pain, and I really didn't mind that it happened.

The flurry who had been tugging at me emitted a series of high-pitched squeals at the other flurries, some of whom stopped their roaming and to listen to it. The flurry was clearly, as Em would put it, *pissed off*. The few others squealed back to it, then rolled over to my leg and began pulling at the cracked pieces, pulling the divots out and trying to smooth out the surface of my leg.

"Thank you," I said to them. "I think I'll be fine, though. I don't much need my leg."

They kept on working, not paying me much attention. When the few of them were finished fixing me up as best they could, they churned in single, small spirals close by me, and I realized that they were guarding me from the other flurries. When the larger packs would get near, my guardian flurries would fly at them and bounce them into another direction.

It all seemed like so much work when I didn't feel like I needed protection, but I sensed that they had found some great sense of purpose in guarding me, and I didn't feel I had the right to take that away from them. Their sense of purpose seemed so focused, so clear and unwavering, and there was an exquisite beauty in it. I felt it resonating in the air around me, and I felt my own purpose inside, that of creating with Em, and these two purposes vibrated in the room together, seemingly making each other stronger. Even in my low-energy state, I could feel my purpose being refined by theirs, like a rock being chipped against another rock to make a weapon or a tool.

And as my guardian flurries' devotion became more defined and pure, the image of me shifted. I was no longer just something to protect – I was a god, a sacred and ancient relic to them – and all their belief and history and culture relied on them protecting me with their lives. Protecting me became their reason for living.

Something happened to all the other flurries in the room as well – their patterns became more complex, evolving so as not to bash against each other or me or the guardian flurries. One pack would all bounce against a wall or the bookcase and arc up through the air, and another pack would circle underneath them before the first pack hit the ground, missing a collision by mere inches.

Earlier I had thought of floating up to the roof to commune with the sunlight, but I was so transfixed on the patterns and evolutions of the flurries, and so tired. I began falling in and out of dreams, and in some of my dreams I understood what the flurries were saying to each other, and I came from the same world that they did. I would watch romances between them, see leaders rise up from among their ranks, waging battles for freedom from other forces that would keep them imprisoned or restrained.

In one of the dreams my body cracked and fell to pieces, an empty city crumbling in on itself from decay and disuse – but from inside the cracks in my broken concrete walls erupted legions of flurries, and I was all of them, and they left the ruins of me, spreading out in all directions until they covered the barren earth, evolving to take on different tasks and purposes, to embody different meanings, multiplying into both similar and unique societies. They became plant life and animal life and person-life, sometimes working together and sometimes warring against each other. Cities rose and cities fell, and in one of these cities was a flurry who worked at a coffee shop and created paintings. One night while painting she split in two, she multiplied, and the two of them would meet each night with the purpose of a higher level of creation than was possible with her being singular. That flurry who came out of her died after a while, and she used the pieces of it and pieces of herself to construct a new flurry, and they too created together for a while. And then one day while she was out, the flurry she'd constructed was sitting on the floor of a room, watching tiny flurries roaming in packs across the floor, and he dreamed of his body as a city falling apart into the sea. From that broken city hoards of flurries emerged, covering the barren planet. Creating societies. Creating life.

I opened my eyes, but the dreams still flooded across my sight. The dreams made me feel so old – like I existed long before time. But I liked how they felt, I liked their stories, so I dipped my head back into the dreams and felt the joy of so many worlds within worlds flooding through me, and I let that joy radiate back into those worlds, like we were feeding each other.

# chapter 41

The morning after hanging out at Red's house, I was wandering through the park before work, kicking leaves and sketching trees. Without letting myself think about what I was doing, I pulled out my phone and called Matt.

"Hi," he answered.

"Hi Matt," I said, my throat suddenly very dry. I hadn't expected him to pick up, and my heart was like a cannon in my chest. "I'm... I'm sorry I haven't called. I was wondering if we could meet up, maybe tonight or tomorrow."

"Sure." He didn't sound very excited by the idea. "I'm free tonight."

"I get off work at five."

"I can meet you there."

"Thanks. I'll see you then."

He hung up. "Thanks?" I repeated, staring down at my phone. "I couldn't have said something nicer than *thanks*?" I clenched my eyes shut to stop a sudden urge to cry. "Stay calm," I whispered. "Just gonna go make some coffee for people and chill the hell out."

The shift was rather uneventful. It was pretty slow, but I spent my extra time doodling in my sketchbook and managed not to worry too much about what to say to Matt, trying to take Red's advice.

After work I met Matt out by the fire pit. I crouched atop one of the broken benches, and Matt stood looking at the fire, his hands in the pockets of his corduroy jacket. The sky was darkening above us. "Oh shit, you're gonna miss your meeting with Om," I said.

He shook his head. "It's alright, she knows."

I took a deep breath and looked into the fire. "Matt, I've been thinking about you a lot. We don't really know each other, but I like you. And I'm a really really fucked up girl. More fucked up than I thought I was. I just didn't realize it because I haven't let myself like someone in a very long time." I looked over at him and he seemed to be deep in thought, but he didn't seem as angry as he'd been when he first walked up. He just stared at the fire.

"If I had known I'd be like this I would have warned you or something," I said. "But I didn't know before, so I'm telling you now. My past... well it's kinda fucked up. Kinda *really* fucked up. And I've got bad blood, too. I've got the crazy gene, or maybe a handful of crazy genes, running through me. And when you held me at the concert, it felt so good. The whole night felt so good. And then all my head parts went crazy all at once." I looked at him again, but he was a statue, just staring at the fire.

He licked his lips. "I don't know what to say."

"You don't have to say anything. I'm sorry I haven't talked to you. Mostly I want to say that I'll need some time. Hopefully not much time. But I can't pull you into this right now, I gotta make peace with some things inside of me first." I closed my eyes and pressed my fingers into my forehead. "And if you're freaked out by me and want to run, I'll understand. Or if you just want to hang out and be friends."

He rubbed his chin, his eyes still on the fire. "We take turns chasing each other away." He looked over at me, and the intensity of his green eyes nearly made me lose my balance. I felt so hollow in their gaze, like a flute. "So what are you going to do, when I start telling you all the reasons that *I'm* weird and fucked up? I mean, it's not as if you like me because I have an overabundance of normalcy." Then he smiled a little.

I smiled back, and then laughed at myself. "I don't know what I'll do. I guess I'll be stuck trying to lighten the mood. I'll probably think, *God, this guy's kinda full of himself, isn't he? Why can't he just hurry up and get his shit together and smile?*"

His smile faded away. "Take care of yourself. And good luck with it all. You'll call me when you're done?"

I nodded.

He looked down at his shoes. "Good. I'll see you, then."

I bit the inside of my lip. "Yeah, I'll see you. I'm gonna sit here for a bit."

He took a deep breath and walked away.

# chapter 42

I looked up from a dream as Em walked in. She tossed her bag onto the floor and flipped off the stereo. I smiled and let out a deep sigh as the flurries all withered away, becoming smaller and smaller until they were like dust and vanished. "Thank you," I whispered to them.

"You look like shit," she said. "You up for tonight?"

The skin under her eyes was red and some of the white had washed out of her hair, leaving it a dark gray like someone pretending to be a ghost. She still hadn't been sleeping much.

"I was just resting up," I told her.

"Good." She pulled the ice cube tray from the freezer. "That's what I like to hear." She turned on some music and made herself a drink.

\*  \*  \*

For hours we danced, and a belief came to me that each and every night Em and I created whole worlds. Worlds full of people and religions and cultures, so many storylines twisted and braided together, like the experience at the concert. But it was not really us creating the worlds, it was her. She created them with the energy that I gave to her, which was energy she'd given to me first that I was just giving back.

These worlds we made, they were born and they thrived and they struggled, then they were washed away, leaving behind their legacy, their story. And that story is what was left sitting on the easel in Em's bedroom each morning.

Halfway through the night I fell away from her, my hollow and thin body hardly making a sound as I hit the floor behind her.

"What's wrong?" she asked, turning to me. "W?"

"I need to rest," I said, holding a hand to my chest. "I'll be alright." My chest burned, but the burning felt good.

She waited, making another drink and pacing the room. She rearranged the paintings leaning against the wall, looking through them. She finished her drink and made another, then leafed through the Klimt book that Matt had given her. I watched her with silent fascination. Even *she* was made of the world, pretending to be Em. She was perfect in every way. The world was pretending to be this perfect creature.

"I'll fucking paint without you," she said, going back to the piece. I watched her work, her movements getting more jagged and uncertain. "Fuck!" she screamed, throwing her glass to shatter against the wall. She grabbed the small painting with one hand and threw it across the room. "What good are you, W!" she yelled at me. "What good are you to me!" She beat her fists against the wall and pointed at the stack of paintings leaning against the wall. "This! This is all I have! It's all I'm good for!"

"Em," I said. I could see no reason at all for her to be upset. Everything was so calm and so simple.

She fell hard onto her knees. "I can't... I can't be here," she cried. She bent forward in front of me until her head touched the cement floor. "I just want to paint. I just want to erase the world and paint. Just erase myself and paint."

Her back heaved up and down as she cried.

"Em," I said.

She looked up at me, her face pink and wet.

"Nothing's wrong," I said, and I smiled. "Nothing's wrong at all."

Confusion crossed her face. "What do you mean?"

"I mean..." I surfed through her thoughts and words, trying to find another way to phrase it. "Everything that's wrong, and everything that's right – it's all bullshit." I reached up and picked a molecule off the wall, watching it flip as I held it between my thumb and forefinger. "See this?"

She nodded. "Yeah."

I motioned around the room. "Everything, the world, it's all just made of these. And these have no meaning. Only the meaning you give them. The meaning that you assign to them with your imagination."

She shook her head and looked slowly around the room. I could see, in the reflection of her eyes, the room breaking apart around us into so many tiny molecules. Tears were still dripping down her face when she began to laugh.

"Son of a bitch," she said. She held her hand out towards the wall and dipped her fingers into it. Then she crawled towards me and lay down with her head in my lap, and I smiled, running my fingers through her hair.

"Thank you," she whispered. "Thank you."

# chapter 43

The sky was white and overcast as Red and I walked along the sandy beach. It was colder out by the lake than it was in the city, and there were only a few boats out. I was picking up rocks that caught my eye and slipping them into my bag. There was an eruption of chirping from the thicket of pine trees behind us, but besides that the only sounds were our sneakers crunching in the sand, the distant hum of boats and the lapping of tiny waves on the beach and rocks.

"I think this is good for you," said Red. She climbed up and stood on a hollow log and started skipping stones on the water. "I mean, all this crap about your dad is in your head anyway, and the more it's uncovered the more you can deal with it. Maybe being close to a guy is what you need. As long as you're sure about him being on the level. And as long as you two take it slow."

I dropped a rock into my bag. "One thing he said to me was that I wouldn't like him if he was normal, and he's right. So I don't know if he's on the level, but I might not like him if he wasn't a bit weird. I have a good feeling about him, though."

"Let's just say that if he hurts you, Em, you'll be more scarred by what I'll do to him than by anything he can do to you."

"I'll let him know."

"So will I, Em. So will I." She jumped down off the log and pulled a piece of paper from her bag. It was a grainy picture printed off the internet.

"What's this?" I said, taking it from her.

"You're not the only girl with boy trouble. The printer at the library sucks, but the online pic is pretty good quality. There's also a video of it."

The picture showed the side of a large abandoned warehouse. There were pictures and symbols painted all over it, and huge piles of wood set aflame in the foreground. In front of the bonfires was a row of five porcelain masks, each one a different color with symbols drawn on them.

"This isn't one of yours, is it?" I asked. Out of all the pictures I'd seen of her work, this one looked very different.

"It's this guy up in Buffalo called 13-K. He's huge in the renegade art scene, and we hung out a lot the last time I was up there. Supposedly he did this nearly all by himself, and it's a *love* letter to yours truly."

"Ooh." I laughed. "Damn, Red! Is he cute?"

She smirked and skipped another stone across the lake. "He's pretty hot."

"You gonna go for it?"

"Yeah. I think the only chance I have at dating someone right now is if they live across the country. And he's definitely got the crazy/weird factor working for him."

"So you haven't talked to him yet?"

"Not yet. Wanted to wait a day or two. Think it over, make him sweat. He'll probably want me to come up there, but I won't go until after the art opening."

"You should have him fly down and be your date."

"Maybe. I'll call him tomorrow. Or maybe I'll just send him some weird conceptual package in the mail that doesn't actually tell him anything. Or send him a computer virus called *I like you too*, or maybe *flowers*. That would be pretty romantic, don't you think?"

"You're asking *me* about romance? Sounds like you're surrounded by it right now."

"You know it." She smiled and threw another stone, then raised her arms to the sky and stretched. "There's only a little over a week left until the opening. It's getting to the point where I won't be able to make new frames in time for the show."

I nodded. "I don't think me and W have much left in us."

"How's he doing?"

"I don't know. He's weak, and can't create for more than a couple hours a night. But he seems happy enough."

"Well, tell me the sizes that you *might* make so I can start prepping some frames."

"I'll figure it out tonight."

Red looked out over the lake. "I just got the strangest urge."

"What's that?"

"I think we should go to the theater, see the worst looking movie there, sit in the front row and throw popcorn at the screen and make jokes."

She turned to me, and I nodded, slowly. "I could... I could do that."

Red shrugged. "Unless we get distracted by something along the way."

I took one last long breath of the fresh lake air, then we started walking back to the road and the bus stop.

*          *          *

The next night I met up with Matt at the park by my house. The park was empty, and I was sitting on one of the playground swings when he walked up.

"Nice night out," I said.

"It is. Especially for being a month into Autumn."

I pulled something the size of a book wrapped in newspaper out of my bag and handed it to him.

"What's this?" he asked.

"A peace offering. Open it."

He sat down on the other swing and opened the package carefully. "A painting... Em, you're giving me a painting?"

I nodded. "I made it for you. You showed me your art, and this is my way of showing you mine."

He held it like a sacred relic in his hands. "It's great. Thank you."

"I've got a lot of work to do before the opening, but I'd like to hang out with you. Maybe the afternoon before the show?"

"Sure. And if you need some fresh air in the middle of the night, any night, give me a call."

"I'll do that."

chapter 44

The barrier between the dream world and the real world had diminished into non-existence. Every time I was in reality, I was partaking of the world's dream. And every time I was dreaming, I was watching the world dream itself through my mind. I no longer knew how many times Em and I had created. The pieces we'd made disappeared as she took them to Red's apartment, so there were never more than two leaning against the wall at any time. I felt something coming, felt the world smirking in anticipation from the walls like some maniac trickster god. All I could do was sit and wait and watch, but that sitting and watching was the only thing I wanted anymore, I was so content. But along with the contentedness, growing with the world's mounting anticipation was a palpable sense of curiosity inside of me. I felt like I was the audience for the world's stage, like the ultimate play was about to be performed for me, and I was so curious as to what the world had planned. Or perhaps the world had none of it planned – this possibility only amplified the curiosity inside.

Em was fast asleep, and dawn would be coming within the hour. We'd only been able to create for a little over an hour that night before I fell to the ground, trembling. She'd been sleeping longer than she had in weeks.

She rose from her bed then, her body wrapped in the night's shadows, and walked across the room. She lit a candle and brought it over to me, sitting it on the ground next to me. I was not surprised to see that this was the other part of Em, the one who had killed my predecessor and pieced me together with parts of him. The candle light played across the skin of her face like hands across the keys of a piano.

"I've been waiting for you," I said.

She put her hand on my shoulder. "I have a task for you," she said. With her lips next to my ear, she whispered what she would have me do. Before she was done, tears were trickling down my face. They dripped gold onto my hollow chest. Without looking, I knew what she'd placed in my palm. She closed my hand and held it between both of hers, as frail and light as they were.

"I do not wish to do this," I said. When she backed away and looked at me, there was such kindness in her eyes. "But I will do anything you ask of me."

"I know," she said.

She moved to sit across from me, placing the candle in between us. We sat there for a long time staring at each other in candle light, until the room began to lighten, stealing away the candle's power. Then the she smiled, blew out the candle and went to lay back down in her bed.

# chapter 45

Inconsequential raised a hand to stop me from speaking. He stood across his desk from me in the office above his shop, Arkan's Vault, in a cream colored suit with the tips of three green and violet feathers sticking out of his breast pocket.

"During every conversation," he said, "I like to make an offering to the spirits of communion. Last time we had tea. This time I was considering a pipe. I have some wonderful scented tobacco, if you'd like to share some with me."

I nodded. "Sure, I'd like that."

"Every conversation is sacred," he said as he prepared the wooden pipes. "And it's good to pay homage to them, and to remind ourselves of their significance." He handed me a pipe and lit a match. "And you know not to inhale the tobacco from a pipe?"

I nodded and puffed on the pipe, pulling the flame into the tobacco. It tasted of clove and honey. "I smoke cigars with a friend of mine."

He raised an eyebrow as he lit his own pipe. "Of course you smoke cigars. What was I thinking?"

I pulled up a chair and we both sat down.

"Alright," he said. "So what is it that's brought your lovely face into such questionable company as mine?"

I handed him a piece of paper. "This is a flier for my show. It's a week from today, in the coffee shop where I work."

"*Spectacle of the Extension and Other Such Illusions*," he read. "*A night of visuals and sound from the minds of the strange. With visual creations by Em and Red and musical...* so on and so forth. Very nice, young lady."

"I was hoping that you'd come. I've seen your work, and I'd love for you to see mine."

He nodded, placing the flier on the table. "It's on the night of the full moon. I think this would be a charming way for me to celebrate."

"Good."

"Now, for the deeper reason that you're here." He puffed on his pipe, the smoke becoming a gray halo around him. "Something is troubling you."

"I have to kill W."

"Yes? He isn't here. Why is that?"

"He doesn't have the energy to follow me around anymore. He barely has the energy to create with me. He's fulfilled his purpose." I puffed on my pipe. I was hollow inside, but wasn't sad or afraid.

"You seem pretty sure of yourself. So what's the problem?"

I looked up and blew smoke towards the ceiling. "You're the only person I can tell who kind of understands."

"Have you talked to Monsieur W about this? Does he understand?"

"He knows, but he doesn't care about things anymore. He's completely fine with anything that could happen – just looks around with this smile on his face, watching everything."

"He's holding on for you. He's waiting for you to let him go."

I leaned forward, looking down at the pipe in my hands. "He is."

"I once had someone who waited for me to let them go." He looked at the painting on his wall, the one with all the people in makeup leaving the dying city. He had said that a woman painted it for him, lifetimes ago. "She waited for quite a while. The doctors were astounded by how long she lasted, but I was not. She would have waited *years* longer if I had demanded it of her. That's the way our love was. That's the way *she* was. Love is a pact, it's a deal. But the deal changes. It is not meant to last through the storms of time, you see, it's an *aspect* of those storms. Love is the wind, the chaos, the peace. It's all of it. You want it to be one thing, just one thing, but it cannot be contained or defined like that for more than a fleeting moment. You cannot just cut a piece of it off and put it into a box."

I smiled. "The way you speak – you don't sound like you're from this world."

"Each of us are from our own separate world. We just pretend to inhabit a single, solitary world."

Turning my head, I blew out a long river of smoke. "About the show – Matt's going to be there."

He looked at me and raised an eyebrow, his bald forehead wrinkling up. "Ah, the boy. You have feelings for him."

"Is it that obvious?"

"When his name flies from betwixt your lips it comes wrapped in hope and butterflies and tiny little hearts painted with glitter."

"Yeah, that makes it sound pretty obvious."

Inconsequential gripped his chest with one hand. "Oh, young love..."

"So, I was wondering... if you might be able to put your dislike of him aside. There's a small chance that he may even be performing. And I'd like for you to come, but I don't want any bad moods floating around."

Inconsequential was silent for a moment, gazing at the painting on his wall. "I come from a place far from here, a place where people like us are trampled on like dust, where people like us are... *encouraged*, to put it nicely, to smother out what makes us tick, what makes us feel alive. Where if people like us do not follow protocol, we are put down like rabid dogs." He turned to me and leaned forward, over the desk. "And why? Why? Because, dear Em, I come from a place where people like you and I are *feared* by the people who run things. Where what we see, what we are, could cause collapse in the very structure of society. In that society, you and I are a disease. A cancer."

"Where? Where are you from?"

He shook his head. "Where I am from is irrelevant for this particular conversation. The fact that it is not obvious is proof that there are too many places that fit the description I give." Smoke rolled out of his mouth like flurries of sound as he puffed from his pipe. "I do not dislike Matt. Not necessarily." Inconsequential closed his eyes. "When I was a boy I saw my friends die or vanish merely for being like you and I – for not hiding who and what they were." He looked down and studied the pipe in his hands. "I should have died coming here, to this country. But something, some force in the universe, spared me. My friends who died were so much more talented than I, so much more amazing and fearless. That's why I'm alive, Em, and not them – I'm alive because I was too much a coward to fully embrace who and what I was. I escaped, and every day since then I remember those friends that I lost, and every day I strive to become as great as I can be, all in their honor."

He turned to me, and the slightest hint of a tear hid in the corner of his eye. "So you see, dear Em, when I see someone like Matt, someone with so much *potential*, living in a country where we can all be what we truly are, and yet he just throws it all to the wind... doing the same drivel over and over, like he's playing it safe. I don't dislike him. I just want him to unlock himself. Do you see?"

I nodded.

"When I look at him, I see myself as a boy. Or I see one of my friends, from so long ago. And I just want to shake him up and tell him that he's not in that horrible place any longer – that he can be free and let go and live."

"I understand what you're saying. But Matt's not your younger self, or one of your friends. And if you've never bothered having a real conversation with him, how do you know he's not being himself? Maybe you should just talk to him."

Inconsequential smirked. "You are quite right, Madame. I will put my judgments aside for the night, as per your request. I may even be conversational with the young lad. As to whether I am wrong about him *not* accessing his potential, we shall see."

"That means a lot to me."

He looked at me and cleared his throat. "I haven't met someone like you in a very long time, so I've let myself ramble on quite a bit. You probably know more about me now than anyone living. It's been a long time since I've felt so comfortable in the presence of another human being."

"Well, thank you for telling me your stories. I feel very honored that you shared so much. And thanks for understanding about Matt." My pipe had gone out, and I placed it on the desk. "I think I'm done smoking."

His pipe was also out. "Oh, to be young and so full of knowledge... I will see you and Matt at your art opening, Madame."

*         *         *

When I got home, it was completely dark. I got some ice from the freezer and started making myself a drink, the whole time listening to W's labored breathing across the room by the paintings. I stood at my kitchen counter and drank the Black Russian in a few drinks, then wiped my mouth with the back of my hand.

My eyes had adjusted to the light, and I crossed the room to where he was sitting between the two large paintings of him. I held out my hand. "I want you to stand up."

He took my hand and I pulled him up and leaned him against the wall. "Did you see Inconsequential?" he whispered. It sounded like it hurt him to talk.

"Yeah, I saw him." I leaned against his shaking body, my cheek against his shoulder. My hands found his sides, and they were so hollow and skinny, but he had no ribs underneath the stretched flesh. He felt like a misshapen drum. "I love you, W."

"I know you do, Em." He placed a hand on the back of my head.

"I'm going to let you go. You don't have to wait for me anymore."

I felt him nod.

Reaching over to my table of paints, my hand fumbled around until it found a thin paint brush. I gripped onto the brush side and took a step back, then brought it between us so the point was at his chest. Taking a deep breath, I leaned towards him with the weight of my body. W slipped to the side and the handle of the brush cracked against the wall and a spasm ran up and down the length of my body. I slouched sideways against the wall and coughed hard. My body felt so strange, like something had been yanked out of it. I shook and my legs went limp, but W held me there against the wall.

"I'm sorry, Em," said W. "I'm so, so sorry."

I looked down and saw my knife in W's hand, the knife I used to cut my hair so that I could sign my paintings, and it was covered in red. There was a dark circle growing on my shirt, over my stomach. The knife clattered to the ground and I collapsed, W too weak to catch me or slow my decent. Then I was staring at the ceiling, and W was looking down on me. I could see his tired gray eyes wanting to cry, but there was nothing left in them. Different parts of my body began shutting down in succession, like a city with rolling blackouts.

The ceiling opened up like a giant cut with white light pouring from it, like an eye looking down on me – an eye of light. I could hear the ceiling and the eye inhale, and it breathed me into it, sucking me up inside until I was surrounded by that light. The light weakened and trickled away, leaving me standing in a very small cement room.

There was a metal desk against the wall, a metal chair and a bed with a very thin mattress. There were things taped up on the wall – a calendar and notes and a picture of the Earth. A man was sitting with his back to me, reading at the desk which held a small pile of books and a notebook. I looked down and there wasn't any blood on me. Maybe I was dead. Maybe this was God, or something like God.

I sniffed and the man spun around. "Jesus Christ!" he yelled. He pulled off his reading glasses. "You scared the shit out of me! Who let you in here?" He looked behind me.

I backed up into a wall of metal bars. "Dad?" I tried to say, but no sound came from my lips.

"Emily," he whispered. He looked so much older, way older than he should have looked. A jagged scar ran across the side of his neck, and his body was larger and more muscular than it had been. He shook his head. "They... they didn't say you were... coming..." His eyes fell to the ground in front of me, and this man who was a stronger, prison-wearied version of my father began to crumble. He hugged himself, his thick fingers digging into the muscles on his arms.

My foot kicked something. I crouched down and picked my knife up from the floor, looked at the clean blade sitting in the palm of my shaking hand. So many images flooded through my mind – memories of my dad, of my nightmares, of feeling my life picked apart as if by vultures.

Inside myself, I plunged my hands deep down into the dark, grabbing hold of another pair of hands, and pulled another me up to the surface. And then I was both myself and that other girl, that other me, looking down at the knife. My body and my heart calmed, but I wasn't burying anything – I wasn't hiding anything from myself.

The man in the chair was like a statue except for his eyes, which were darting all around the floor, then up at the knife in my hand, then back at the floor. His face contorted until it looked like one of the sad drama masks. "I... I don't know why they let you in here..."

"You know no one let me in here." My voice was different, rising up from deep inside, feeling like something much older than I was.

"Wha... why've you come? I wish... I wish you hadn't..."

"Why?" I said, shaking my head. "*Why*."

He strained to look me in the eyes. "I'm so many... there are really bad things... things I can't fight. I tried to be normal, Emily. I tried so hard. With a family, a desk job. And I had enough strength to protect you from the things inside. *I'd never let those parts of me even look at you!*" A stream of drool dripped down his chin and onto the floor. "You're the only thing that ever *meant* anything to me. Everything else was a charade, but you were real. *I* was a charade! But I had so much strength around you, so much strength. I thought maybe, maybe I'd overcome it because of you."

There were tears on my cheeks, but I didn't feel like I was crying yet. "Why did you have to love me? Why did you make me love you, when you knew what you were?"

"I... I thought you'd save me," he whispered. His eyes looked so tired, so close to death. They had lost their color, fading to the color of ash.

I looked down at the knife in my hand. "I will never forgive you, but you can no longer be a part of me. I'm going to let go of you. I need my heart for other things, and you can't have it anymore. Even if I'm dead now, I don't care. My heart is mine."

He sniffed and nodded, his eyes distant. My hand closed over the knife's handle as I approached. He looked up at me like I was the angel of death, come to release him from his heavy life. I grabbed some strands of my hair and sawed them off with the knife, then sprinkled the gray and black strands on the desk. "Look at this when I'm gone, and know that this visit did happen." I pulled some hair at the top of his head – it was dark gray – and I cut it off. I backed away, looking down at him, the clump of his hair in one hand and the knife in the other. "I'm taking this."

He shook his head. "Emily, I..."

Our eyes met and there were no more words. Silence emanated from the walls, making the room seem to grow. The objects in the room and the walls themselves were hollow inside, and they too yearned to die. Seeing him there, so small in the room full of hollow things, I felt such a calm come over me. The world was pulling at me, beckoning me to go to where I belonged, though I no longer knew where that would be.

And then I was back in my room, standing in the center of it, and all was dark. I set the bloody knife on my paint table and put my father's hair in an empty jar. I pulled off my blood-stained shirt and threw it in the trash, then grabbed a towel to stop the bleeding. W looked up at me as I knelt down beside him in my bra, still holding the towel against my stomach. His voice came in long wheezes, and I knew he could no longer even speak as he lay there.

I remembered things that the other part of me had done now, because that part was not closed off from the rest of me. Not anymore. I remembered giving W the knife, and asking him to do what he did. "Thank you for that last part," I said. "It means the world to me."

His skin was dry and cracked like peeling paint. My hand left a thin smear of blood on his cheek when I touched him. I leaned down and kissed him and his body collapsed into itself underneath me. The world around me, my room, gave out a long, relaxed sigh. The black and golden dust rose up into the air and the room began to lighten with the approach of dawn, the dust catching the light and reflecting it like glitter.

chapter 46

# chapter 47

The wound was not deep, at least not anymore. It hurt when I turned certain ways, but I wasn't going to bother getting stitches. Hospitals reminded me of prison, and of people hurting others. I cleaned the wound and wrapped it, using a towel and masking tape before walking to the store to get proper bandages. My eyes burned from the sun when I walked outside, but it was a good burn. After I'd gotten back home and patched myself up properly, I made coffee and took a cup with me to the park. The park was empty, and I sat among the trees for a while, just listening to them and to the sun and the cold breeze. Then I walked around, collecting small branches and bird feathers.

When it was late enough and I knew she'd be awake, I called Red.

"Yo," she answered.

"Morning," I said.

"You sound weird, what's up?"

"I'll explain in detail later. I'm alright, though. I'm very much alright." I smiled and leaned back against a tree.

"Good, good. So what's shakin', bacon?"

"I've got one more piece. I'm going to need a frame, about two-by-four. It doesn't have to be exact, because there won't be a canvas. I'll need it soon though, because I'm going to attach things to it. Even if you just want to solder together stuff you have lying around, I think that would work."

"Alright, that brings it into the realm of possible. I'll have something there tomorrow, but it might not be pretty."

"Sounds perfect. And do you still have that plaster lying around?"

"Yeah, somewhere."

"Can I come by today and grab it?"

"Of course."

"Maybe around noon?"

"I'll have the Bloody Mary's ready. Just kidding. Kind of. No, wait. Wait. Actually now that I've said it, it's become reality. I will indeed have the Bloody Mary's ready."

\*             \*             \*

Back at my apartment, I spread out the sticks and feathers, along with the stones I'd gotten from the lake. The two paintings of W looked down on the cluster of items. I took out my phone and called Matt.

"Hi, Em," he answered.

"Matt. How are you?"

"I'm doing alright. Was up all night working on a new song."

"That's great." I walked over to my window, pulled the curtain aside and opened it. "I know we haven't talked any more about the art opening, and if you don't want to play I understand. But I was wondering if you would go there with me, and if I could take you to dinner before."

"Um... yeah, I'd like that. I've been working with Om, and we've put together a set list of ten songs."

"You're going to play?"

"If that's still alright."

"Of course it's alright, Matt. Thank you so much!"

"And I want to show you one of the songs, hopefully this week sometime."

"I'm going to be busy getting ready most of the week, working on one last piece." I tongued the inside of my cheek. "What about tonight? I can't be out all night, though. Say yes before I realize it's stupid for me to go out and change my mind."

"Yes."

"Alright, I'll see you tonight."

"Um, seven-ish?"

"Seven-ish it is."

chapter 48

# chapter 49

The sun hadn't set and the evening wasn't that cold yet, and the air that slipped into The Cove through the open doors and windows kissed my face and arms. Red and I had just finished hanging the last of the pieces, and Matt was in the corner setting up his crates and wine glasses while Red lit up a cigar at one of the outside tables. Looking around at the walls all adorned in my paintings and Red's elaborate frames, I could see the story of the two W's splayed out for anyone to see - their evolution, and mine. It was still an hour until the official start of the art opening, and there were only a few customers scattered about the shop, most of them busily pecking away at their laptops.

Matt blushed when he noticed me approaching. He wore a dark green button up with a thin black tie, and I stood next to him and entwined my arm around his. I wore a sleek black dress that I'd years ago adorned with thin strips of Egyptian fabric around the neck and high sleeves and at the bottom, depicting ankhs and the eye of Ra and hieroglyphs. I'd made my hair all spiky, and it was dark black again except for the bangs which were bright red now.

Matt set down the jug of water he was using to fill the wine glasses.

"You need any help?" I asked.

He shook his head. "I'm pretty much done. You should save your energy for all your adorning fans."

I leaned into him and put my head on his shoulder. "I'm only saving myself for one of my fans."

He took my hand in his and our fingers locked. "I really like the red in your hair."

I smirked and pulled away, looking into his dark green eyes. "You found a reason to complement me for a fifth time tonight. A girl could almost think you have a thing for her."

"The red in your hair has a story," he said, peering from my eyes to my red bangs.

"Perhaps I'll tell it to you. Probably soon."

"What you said at dinner – you were right. You are different."

My hand tightened around his. "And what do you think about that?"

"Well, I can tell it's real. Like you're more yourself. You're happier, and I like it. I like different."

I leaned up and pressed my cheek against his. "And different likes you too. A lot." Then I closed my eyes and gave him a long kiss on the cheek. I pulled away and smiled at him, wiping the lipstick off his cheek with my thumb. "I'll let you get back to work. 'Cause if I stay here I'm gonna end up getting my lipstick all screwed up."

"And we couldn't have that."

"Oh, hell," I said and kissed his lips, my eyes slipping shut as our bodies melted against each other. My heart inverted itself and expanded out through my transparent body, expanding so fast that it exploded out into the air around us like stars in the galaxy, the whole of the coffee shop pulsing with its sporadic, throbbing beats. I took a deep breath and pulled away, my heart imploding back into me, and there was so much life flowing through my body. It was my life that flowed through me, it was Em flowing through Em, me flowing through me. I felt so... so *large*. So big. Like I physically occupied more space, like I *was* the space around myself. Like the place where I stopped and where reality started was no longer solidly defined.

I opened my eyes, saw Matt and burst out laughing, then covered my mouth with my hand, remembering all the customers in the shop. I covered Matt's mouth with one hand and grabbed a napkin from Matt's table, dipped it into one of his water-filled wine glasses and wiped the smudges of lipstick off his lips. When he realized what I was doing he cracked up too.

"I have to stop getting cheap lipstick," I said. "My lips look horrible too, I suppose."

He shook his head. "Not so bad."

I nodded. "And in guy-speak that means my lips look ridiculous." I twisted my mouth at him. "I'm gonna go fix them, and let you get back to setting up your symphony. And tell Om I say hi."

"You can tell tell her yourself," he said, nodding beside me. It was then that I realized that the sun was setting, so Matt would be able to see her.

I looked over, and for a split second I thought I saw the air shimmering in the corner. My eyes darted back to Matt and I raised my eyebrows. "Oh?" I said, then glanced back at the corner and whispered. "Hi, Om! Good luck, I'm looking forward to everything!" And when I squinted I could actually see her star-filled eyes staring at me from the shadows, and the eyes widened. She knew that I could see her. I pressed my hand to my heart and nodded. I was no longer scared of what she knew about me. Actually, I was no longer scared of anything, it seemed.

I backed up and curtsied towards Matt as best I could in the thin dress, then darted into the bathroom, fixed my lipstick, then grabbed my jean jacket and went outside. The air was so warm and perfect for the middle of fall, the kind of mid-autumn weather that made everyone go out in hoards and flock to events, so hopefully people would show up tonight.

Red was nearly done with her cigar, crouched and sitting atop the back of one of the metal chairs in her tattered khaki pants and leather jacket, with a white shirt with a big bull's eye drawn on it all Tank Girl style. "Think I might hurl," she said.

"Oh?" I said, swiping the cigar from between her fingers and taking a drag, carefully so as not to mess up my lipstick too much. "Didn't think you were the type to get nervous."

"Nervous? It's not nerves. But with you and your boy all lovey-dovey and shit –"

"Pshh," I muttered and flipped her off, and she immediately cracked up.

"No, no, of course I'm kidding," she said. "I mean, it's pretty nauseating, sure, but I can swallow it, you know, shove it back down, since I've never seen you fucking happier in your life." She licked her lips. "I don't even know if I should say this, but I just hope it's not a phase. I hope you're getting that happiness from yourself, not just from dreams of him or something."

"It's from me," I said, glancing back through the windows at Matt setting up his wine glasses. I puffed from the cigar and handed it back to Red. "It's all from me, and I keep almost crying, to tell the truth. Not from being sad, but from feeling more free than I've ever felt in my life. Does that make sense?"

"Gods," said Red. "You're gonna get *me* teary-eyed, girl."

I smiled at her. "Matt's just extra. I mean, I don't think I'll tell him that. Not yet, after all I've put him through. But I'm genuinely happy, just by myself, and then there's Matt, and he makes me even happier."

Red blew a stream of smoke out through a smirk. "That is so good to hear. But that whole killing-him-if-he-hurts you promise is still in effect, just for the record."

"Dually noted."

She nodded behind me and Matt walked out and up to our table.

"Finished setting up?" I asked, and he nodded.

"How's it going, Red?" he asked.

"Sure," she said. "That'll be three eighty-five, please." She shook her head and feigned a sudden realization. "Oh, shoot, I was expecting you to say *medium latte*. Sorry, um, Matt. I'm doing pretty freaking good. Thanks for asking."

I sighed loudly. "Red, please play nice."

"I only play one way," she said, hopping down to the ground and sticking her hand out to Matt. "Sir Matt, pleased to officially meet you."

He reached out and shook her hand. "Your work is amazing," he said. "I mean it. You could have a whole separate art show and just show those frames."

"That might be weird," she said. "An art show with empty frames."

He nodded. "Weird, but you could pull it off."

"You're damned right I could." She gripped his hand and pulled him closer, eyeing him up and down. "You know that if you harm Em, I will harm you to an exponentially higher degree? And that no amount of flattery will change that one iota?"

He nodded, unflinching (I'd warned him, of course).

Red released his grip and nodded. "Well, alright then." She sat back and plopped her boots onto onto one of the neighboring chairs, motioning to an empty chair. "Please, sit for a spell and tell me about yourself, Sir Matt. Let us exchange stories and artistic visions."

Somehow he seemed to know that he'd been accepted by Red the same moment that I myself knew, and he pulled out a chair and took a seat at the table. I almost felt like he was drawing from my own energy, my own confidence, but I couldn't be sure. Maybe he was confident because of a change in himself, or a change between himself and Om. Just the idea that I would find out more about this young man and what he was going through filled me with such joy and wonder that my whole body vibrated with it.

Red looked at me and motioned to an empty chair. "Join us."

"I could," I said. "But I was thinking about getting the wine ready."

She pointed at me with the cigar. "Yes, wine. Wine is important. Helps the creativity, uh... flow."

Just then I saw someone walking up through all the broken post-apocalyptic buildings of The Island. I smirked. It was Inconsequential, in a chartreuse suit. "Oh, thank you for coming!"

"Of course, Madame," he said. "I said I would, did I not? I'm not so good with crowds, I'm afraid, so I came a bit early. I wanted to get a good look at the artwork before others arrived and proceeded to rudely block my view."

"Well, I'm not actually sure that so many people are coming."

Inconsequential pulled back the sleeve of his suit coat and glanced at his wristwatch. "Oh, they're on their way – don't kid yourself about that. Humans have a way of intuiting when something real, some genuine movement, is taking place, and they instinctively want to be there when it does, because they know it affects the whole."

His words took me by surprise, since he hadn't even seen my work yet. Then I turned to the table. "I believe you already know Matt."

Inconsequential stuck out his hand. "Not formally, I'm afraid," he said, and when Matt hesitantly stuck out his hand, Inconsequential grabbed it and shook it firmly. "Monsieur Matt, it is a great pleasure to finally meet you. It seems I was a bit of a child and an old man in the past, and I hope that you can overlook my... flaws and misperceptions." He smiled a wrinkly smile. "You will too be old and young someday, and will have plenty such instances for which to apologize, I'm sure."

Matt nodded. "Good to meet you," he said, though I could tell he was a bit skeptical.

"And I so look forward to your performance," said Inconsequential, and his words were so genuine that it even shocked me a little. Something in him had turned, and when he said those words it was almost as if he wanted to see Matt perform more than he wanted to see my artwork. And the knowledge of that filled me with so much joy, and not the tiniest bit of jealousy.

Then the man turned to Red. "Bonjour, Madame, I am Inconsequential. Humbly at your service."

Red tonged the inside of her cheek so that it bulged out, then reached out with the hand that wasn't holding the last bit of cigar. "Red," she said. "Knight in shining armor, frame maker, photographer extraordinaire, rebel, anarchist, et cetera, et cetera."

"Indeed," said Inconsequential, who took her hand in his and kissed the top of it. "Pleased to meet you."

"And how do you know Em?" she said, at which point I realized I'd never mentioned him to her. So many things had gone on in my life and in my head that even though he was so interesting, he seemed so periphery.

He glanced at me and said, "You know – I could tell the most adventurous stories of our first encounter. But in reality I'm merely a boring old man who this lovely lady happened upon one day."

"Yeah, I'm sure that's how it went," said Red, looking at me suspiciously.

"Madame," said Inconsequential, taking Red's attention away from me. "I beg your pardon, but there is something right there on your forehead." He motioned to the center of his own forehead with a finger, but I couldn't see anything on Red's face. "Just a tiny speck, but it's oh so distracting."

Red raised an eyebrow and wiped her forehead slowly as if she thought he was pulling some silly prank on her, then shook her head.

Inconsequential's eyes widened and he leaned towards her. "Oh..."

"Oh?" she asked, playing along.

Then, completely seriously, he said, "It's a piece of the universe, stuck there right between your eyes." He pointed at her forehead, then nodded. "You might want to see to that."

I expected Red to come back with some witty response, but she just stared blankly at Inconsequential, almost as if she'd just realized that she knew who he was, or as if he'd told her something extremely important.

Inconsequential stood up straight, brushed off his jacket and motioned to the doors of The Cove. "Well, I'd better see what this is all about, before everyone else arrives. If the three of you would excuse me." He made a short bow and wandered into the coffee shop.

Red touched her forehead, and looked so contemplative, as if he'd told her some kind of scientific formula and her mind was going through all the calculations, switching out all the variables and trying to decipher its meaning. Then she shrugged it off and looked up at me. "Why are you still out here? Your first guest is inside. Go show him around!"

"Yeah, I should." I squeezed Matt's shoulder, then went inside.

Inconsequential was slowly moving from piece to piece, so I went to the wine table and uncorked a few bottles of red. I grabbed two wine glasses from behind the counter (so that I didn't have to give him wine in a plastic cup), and poured us a couple of glasses.

"Wine?" I asked, stepping up beside him. "As an offering to the spirits of communion?"

"Yes, of course. Thank you." He motioned around at the paintings on the walls. "They are all in chronological order."

"You can tell?"

"Usually not the best way to display a series of pieces, but in this case it works well. The energy flows through them quite remarkably. Well done, Madame Em." He took his glass from me and raised it. I tapped mine against his. "To creation and its effects on us and on the world."

We both drank. "Now this piece," he said, pointing to it with his wine glass. "Obviously the last piece created. I haven't yet taken a good look at it – but very interesting, Madame."

"Thank you."

He began looking over the piece. The "frame" I'd made from branches I'd found in the park, and it was more of a found-object sculpture, with no paint involved at all. There were twigs and leaves and vines that I'd woven together across the middle of it, and stones and feathers hung from the bottom of it like wind chimes. In the center was a mask of my face, but facing into the piece, so that only the inside of the mask was showing – like it was inviting the onlooker to step up and press their face into my own. Two weeks ago that idea would have scared the shit out of me – to invite a stranger to put on my face and look through my eyes, to be inside my head. But not anymore.

Below the mask hung a small mason jar with a lock of my

father's gray hair inside. And from behind the whole piece a conglomeration of twisted metal scraps radiated out in spikes like a star.

I sipped my wine nervously, but kept myself from drinking too much of it. I didn't want to be too buzzed during the opening.

"My, oh my," said Inconsequential, nodding. "I'd like to hear the story about this piece one day, if you'd be so kind as to grace me with it."

"I think that can be arranged. You haven't... you haven't asked me about W."

He turned his head and looked me up and down. "Any questions I had about Monsieur W, as tiny as they were, were whisked away the moment I got here."

I nodded, and he turned back to the piece.

"One thing I find quite interesting," he said, "is the manner in which you signed the piece. The other ones are so very similar to each other. But not this one." He pointed down to the bottom tree branch. "But I suppose that comes along with the story of the piece."

"I suppose it does," I said, sipping my wine.

I was the forest. I was the rain.

Moving between the trees, through the overgrowth, I could smell my prey on the tips of the wind's hair. I could taste the sweet flesh at the edges of my teeth, could feel the adrenalin laced in the dirt between my toes as I ran. My body soaked, my heart drenched, my eyes aflame. I stopped paying attention to the trickles of blood left on passing leaves and branches – I was so close now that the trail of blood was useless.

Then I saw it there ahead of me – a shadow in the pouring rain, darting past the trees and over renegade roots in search of a miracle. But I was the only miracle in that forest, and I would not be sparing its life.

My prey tripped and fell, rolling instantly back onto its feet to continue running. But in that tiny moment, that little flicker of space, all chance folded into itself as my body collided against it. We surfed through the air, our bodies soaked and covered in my prey's blood, and when we tumbled to the ground and I looked down into my prey's eyes, I saw her looking up at me like I was an incarnation of heaven come to take her soul away. Like she'd been waiting for me.

Reaching down with bloody hands, I ran them slowly through the front of her hair, staining it. Her body relaxed below me, sinking into the mud, her eyes glazing over. Then I grabbed the front of my own hair, pulling the blood through it until it too was crimson.

I reached up and touched the mask that covered my face. As my prey's lifeblood thinned with the pouring rain and mixed into the mud around my bare knees and feet, I pulled the mask off and away *from my face. No longer crouched above my prey in the forest, I was now standing in a small room. On the wall before me was a square conglomeration of branches and leaves and feathers and twine. I tied the mask to the middle of the square of branches.*

*Reaching up to my chest, I grabbed the mason jar hanging from my neck and pulled it over my head, then tied it to the mask so that it hung below it. Inside the jar were strands of dark gray hair.*

*I pulled a knife from my belt, licked my lips. From the top of my head I cut off a thin length hair, smeared it with the blood from the back of my hand. Then, pressing the strands of hair against one of the branches, I wrote my name.*

# Acknowledgments

I would like to thank everyone who has enjoyed my work over the years – those who encouraged me, those who inspired me or were inspired by my strange tales.

A special thank you to my friends Zachary W. Mohr and Caitlyn Watson, who have read this book multiple times while helping me edit, always giving me ideas on how to make my strange visuals clearer to the reader.

And to you, reader, I hope this tale inspires you to spend more time (much more time, perhaps) seeking out the ways in which you'd like to be creative and have a positive, beautiful effect on the world.

Andy Reynolds was a gambler born in New Orleans in 1898. He lived a very messy yet deliberate life, and despite surviving numerous brushes with yellow fever, died quite young in 1936 – an event involving at least one street magician, five insidious cats and a stained glass window. Three incarnations later and he again resides in New Orleans, this time as a writer of fiction and an imbiber of whiskey and local knowledge.

Find out more about his writings at: AndyReynolds.net
& also: Facebook.com/AndyWritings

Read tiny slices of his poetry: Twitter.com/AndyWritings

Watch & listen to him read poems and other such things on YouTube, on his Channel called AndyWritings.

www.ingramcontent.com/pod-product-compliance
Lightning Source LLC
Chambersburg PA
CBHW051638260626
47170CB00004B/1234